The Best
Short Stories
of
Frank Norris

THE BEST
SHORT STORIES
OF
FRANK NORRIS

IRONWEED PRESS
NEW YORK

Ironweed Press, Inc.
P. O. Box 754208
Parkside Station
Forest Hills, NY 11375

Printed on acid-free paper in the United States. This book meets
the guidelines for permanence and durability of the Committee
on Production Guidelines for Book Longevity of
the Council on Library Resources.

Jacket photograph courtesy of Culver Pictures, New York.

Library of Congress Catalog Card Number: 98-71892

ISBN:0-9655309-1-4

CONTENTS

ACKNOWLEDGEMENT

The editor would like to gratefully acknowledge the generous help of Professor Dennis Skiotis of Harvard University; Leslie Morris, Curator of Manuscripts in the Harvard Library; Helen Rand of Interlibrary Services at the University of California at Berkeley; Irene McDermott of San Marino Public Library; Allen Reuben of Culver Pictures, New York; and the staff of New York Public Library.

INTRODUCTION

Frank Norris was born in Chicago on March 5, 1870. Norris's family was well-to-do; his father was a successful businessman, his mother a former stage actress. In 1884 the Norrises moved to California and lived for a brief time in Oakland before settling in San Francisco. At seventeen Norris quit high school to study painting and enrolled at the San Francisco Art Association and then later at the Bouguereau Studio of the Julien Academy in Paris. After his two-year stay in Paris, Norris returned home in 1889. His interest, however, had shifted from art to literature, and Norris soon began his first work, *Yvernelle* (1892), a book-length narrative poem set in medieval France.

In 1890 Norris was admitted to the University of California at Berkeley, where he discovered the works of the French novelist Émile Zola, whose naturalism was to be the foundation of Norris's most important novels. After spending a year studying composition at Harvard, he went to Africa as a correspondent for the *San Francisco Chronicle* and was expelled by the Boers from South Africa as a result of his involvement in the abortive Jameson Raid. The following year he joined the staff of a small San Francisco-based journal called *The Wave*, to which he contributed weekly.

His novel *Moran of the Lady Letty*, serialized in *The Wave* in 1898, caught the attention of the publisher S. S. McClure. McClure called Norris to New York and gave him a job as an editorial assistant on *McClure's Magazine*. In New York Norris came to know William Dean Howells, the influential novelist and critic. Howells, after reading the manuscript, encouraged Norris to publish *McTeague* (1899), a work which Norris had actually written before *Moran of the Lady Letty*. Inspired by a real-life murder at a San Francisco kindergarten, *McTeague* created a welter of controversy; readers and critics alike were scandalized by its subject matter as well as its grim and unflinching realism. But with Howell's vigorous praise, *McTeague* survived the initial negative outcry and ultimately established Norris as one of the pioneering practitioners of literary naturalism.

Norris began work on his ambitious trilogy, titled "The Epic of Wheat," in 1899. The trilogy was to be comprised of *The Octopus, a Story of California*; *The Pit, a Story of Chicago*; and *The Wolf, a Story of Europe*. "When complete," Norris wrote, "they will form the story of a crop of wheat from the time of its sowing as seed in California to the time of its consumption as bread in a village in Western Europe." *The Octopus* was published in 1901 to great critical acclaim. The novel was, in part, an exposé on the corrupt practices of the wheat and railroad trusts, and stands today as one of the best works in "muckraker" literature. The second part of the trilogy, *The Pit* (1903), was based on Joseph Leiter's attempt to corner the Chicago wheat market in 1897. Shortly after the completion of the novel, Norris died of peritonitis on October 25, 1902.

Though his career spanned only eleven years, Norris left behind a substantial body of work. He wrote seven novels and numerous fiction and nonfiction pieces for various magazines and journals. His collected works, published in 1928, total some ten volumes. Today, however, Norris is thought of primarily as a novelist, and what has been largely forgotten is that he was also a prolific and sometimes brilliant short-story writer.

In total, Norris wrote over 60 pieces of short fiction. The majority of his earlier stories was published in *The Wave* and *The Overland Monthly*. Toward the end of his career, his stories appeared regularly in the more-prominent, national magazines, such as *Collier's Weekly* and *Everybody's Magazine*. Posthumously, a number of his short stories were reprinted in three collections: *A Deal in Wheat* (1903), *The Third Circle* (1909), and *Frank Norris of "The Wave"* (1931).

The quality of his short stories varied. A good number of them were potboilers, written to accommodate the popular tastes of his day, and would seem perhaps thin and formulaic to today's readers. But Norris also wrote some wonderfully crafted short stories and would have undoubtedly had a more significant output had his career not been so tragically abbreviated.

When writing short fiction, Norris allowed himself more latitude in subject matter and style. Though not regarded as a humorist, he wrote several comic gems, such as "Buldy Jones, *Chef de Claque*" and "The Dual Personality of Slick Dick Nickerson." His stories of the American West, most of which were set in the mining region of the northern Sierras, also evidenced his comic brio, but as demonstrated in "A Memorandum of Sudden Death," Norris was equally capable of using the Western motif for more substantive and dramatic purposes.

The stories in this collection are arranged chronologically by year and, to a certain extant, chart Norris's maturation as a writer. A few of the stories echo his longer works. "The Jongleur of Taillebois," written when Norris was twenty-one, has the same medieval backdrop as *Yvernelle*, and portions of "Man Proposes No. II" and "Judy's Service of Gold Plate" later resurface in *McTeague*. But, as a body, his short stories stand independent of his novels, revealing the remarkable breadth of his narrative voice. When one reads his short fiction, one realizes that Norris was, above all, a storyteller, one whose generous and varied talents do not readily lend themselves to be subsumed by such academic labels as "naturalist" and "muckraker."

The Best
Short Stories
of
Frank Norris

THE JONGLEUR OF TAILLEBOIS

Now that the heat and excitement of the first attack was over Amelot saw that he had not struck with sufficient precision, and that his sword, glancing from Yéres's head, so quickly averted to avoid it, had only lighted upon and laid open the base of the neck behind the collar bone. But it was enough. If not precise, the blow had been powerful, and Amelot perceived with satisfaction that the gash in Yéres's neck was large enough to let the life out of any man.

It was only a question of time, and so, stepping back to avoid Yéres's furious rolling and tumbling, he waited. He had never killed a man before, and so the sight of one in his agony of violent death was to *his* mind a novel and interesting sight. He watched it with great curiosity. When his first arbalist had been put into his boyish hands, his trial exploit had been the killing of the cat belonging to the wife of his father's seneschal; death had not been instant, and for half an hour the creature howled and writhed. He was reminded of this now as Yéres twisted and rolled back and forth on the ground at his feet, now on his breast, now on his back, now on his hands and knees, and stupidly running his head against the boles of the tree roots. He streaked his clothes and face with his own blood, the dead leaves stuck to his wet cheeks, and the underlying dust was churned into ruddy mud by the quick, incessant opening and closing of his fingers. He uttered no cry, but his tongue protruded and his eyes were fixed and staring.

The precise moment of death Amelot never knew; the spasms and torsions became intermittent, and after a pause longer than usual he concluded life to be extinct, yet he stabbed the body with his *misericordia* to make doubly sure, and stabbed it in a manner peculiarly and significantly his own. He did not *strike* it into the corpse, lest the haste of the blow should again disturb the correctness of the aim, but calculated with nicety the location of the heart, placed the point of his poniard over it and threw his weight upon the haft; the skin dinted beneath the point, then suddenly parted, the blade sunk in up to the hilt, and Amelot rose again with the assurance that his enemy was, beyond doubt, dead.

His first thought now was to conceal the body. He looked about him. He was in the heart of one of those New Forests which his most dread lord, *Wilhelmus Conquestor, Dei Gratiae Rex Anglicorum,* following in the footsteps of his Norman ancestry, was at that moment planting throughout conquered England. The growth of the great oaks, pines, and sycamores was too slow to suit the royal patience and pleasure, and the commissioners charged with the forest extension had been commanded to take up trees of sufficient size from other parts of the island and to transplant the same to those tracts set aside for the kingly hunting grounds. Not far from the spot on which Amelot stood, one of these trees, a mighty black pine, lay upon rollers where it had been dragged by the foresters, and on account of the lateness of that day left to be erected upon the next. Close to where its roots, like enormous tentacles, writhed themselves helplessly into the air had been excavated the circular hole which was to receive them. It was a pit; to Amelot's eyes a grave—a grave for Yéres. Beneath that gigantic trunk what possibility of the body's recovery? Never a grave more closely guarded, never a monument more securely immutable.

The shovels and mattocks of the serfs lay about upon the dirt heaps. He swung himself into the hole, and with them dug to the depth of six or eight feet. "A pit within a pit," he said, smiling, "a secret hid within another."

When he had excavated to what he deemed sufficient extent, he rolled up Yéres in his *chappe* and slid him into the hole, face downward; but life was not yet wholly quenched; one of those strange after-spasms seized upon the body, a muffled sound came from the folds of the *chaperon,* where the face lay pressed against the earth. The whole form twisted itself over upon its back, the cloak was drawn from the mouth, and, as though terrified at the first touch of the great reclaiming mother, from behind the black

lips and clenched teeth there burst a dreadful cry. With a movement quick as the impulse which originated it, Amelot set his foot
upon the mouth and shot his glance down the glooming vistas of
the forest trunks, and strained his ears to catch any possible
answering sigh or sound of succor; but the cry was without
response, and he finished the interment without further interruption. He stamped the earth down over the new grave, raked into
a pile and burned such leaves as were stained with a red that was
not of the autumn, cast his eyes about him, then, in a sudden
panic, fled terror-stricken from the spot.

The next day the serfs of Taillebois planted the Black Pine in
its destined position, where it grew and thrived for fifteen years.

It was raining in the New Forest.

Rain upon the sea, upon an Irish peat moor, in a Scotch post-
ing house, or in a new town in western Kansas, is bleak and desolate enough, but for the very nadir of depression the ultimate
quintessence of dreariness look to a rainy forest at the close of an
autumn afternoon, when the drops drum, drum, drum with incessant monotone upon every shaking leaf, when the green mosses
and tree lichens grow big and spongy with wet, and the thick bark
of the larger trunks turns black with the water and swells to the
consistency of muck, when every tiny, rattling cataract of rain
finds its way into nethermost corners of the undergrowth and
wakes up the drowsy woodland odors asleep between the layers
of dead and fallen leaves; odors which, like heavy incense for
dead and dying nature, steam upward into the silent air, when
everything is quiet and hushed, when the robins sit voiceless on
each secluded bough, fluffing out their feathers, making themselves larger, dozing with their beaks upon their breasts; when
the hart, the boar, and the rabbit, and all the myriad insect life,
are drowsing in their farthest corners, and all is very quiet, while
the drumming of the rain, in endless minor cadence, unceasingly
goes on.

So in that dreamy Twelfth Century forest the gentle rain
purred on all day in dull and muffled cadence, and in the failing
light of the afternoon the wind came softly stealing up.

But with the latest twilight there came a sudden change. A
sharp puff of western wind in an instant dissipated all the lone-

some quiet which since dawn had reigned supreme. The rain ceased, and a great voice passed among the higher foliage, whispering "sh-sh-sh," after which the trees stood upright, silent, and, as it were, expectant, listening for the storm that was to come.

It came. In the utter stillness following upon the first heralding gust could be heard, seemingly, unfathomably below the line of the far horizon, the bell-toned ripple of the distant thunder; then the swish and roar of the rain sweeping the uplands, and at intervals, like the opening and closing of a great eye, came the dull and distant glare of the lightning; all as yet so far away.

But it was getting nearer. With a deafening grating, as of the crash and grind of chaotic worlds, the thunder slid upward toward the zenith; like the zigzag course of some Devil-driven spirit, the lightning shot across the gloom, while with a roar, drowned only by the thunderpeals, the rain rushed down upon all frightened nature. The wind lashed across the open spaces between the trees and over their plunging crests, whipping the forest till, as though racked with pain, it groaned and growled again, tearing up the fallen leaves from the ground and sending them whirling and scurrying about like excited rabbits. Simultaneously all the elements were loosed; tortured antics and violent action rudely usurped the so-recent dreamy repose, and the silence and solitude were broken by all the clash and jar of the tempest. A bad night. For those travellers coming eastward from over the old Watling Street, journeying downward to the Surrey lands, a bad night, indeed.

Of such in this wild October storm Amelot found himself the only representative. As he reined in his tired, fretful Flammand upon the broad, grooved flagging of the Watling Street, in which his reversed reflection was beginning to form, he considered that a bypath leading to the castle, or rather manor, of Taillebois was, in those days when he was a guest in it, wont to turn off not far from the spot upon which his Flammand's feet were then so restlessly shifting and stamping. He should know the country well; fifteen years ago, before the extension of the New Forest and the establishment of the forest laws, he had flown his hawk and lain his hounds in these very glades. It was hereabouts his early life had been passed; along that path he had ridden in gambison and lorica to meet Norman William and to fight and flee at Hastings.

It was here he had first known Yéres. It was here—— By St. Guthlac, enough of that! He crossed himself devoutly. Let the past guard well its own secrets; pilgrimages and offerings would atone.

With little difficulty he found the familiar path, and leading his horse by the bridle entered into the wildly tossing forest on foot. The storm was now at its height, and it was only by the closest scrutiny and surest footing that he managed to follow the devious windings of the trail. On a sudden the tempest rose to hurricane pitch, crash following flash with the regularity and ferocity of a cannonade; his horse pivoted about on his haunches and, shaking free his head, plunged back into the underbrush; hollowest noises raged in the dark upper spaces of the air and were reverberated along the darker cavernous aisles of the tree trunks; the rain became a cataract, the wind a tornado. Battered against the quivering trunks and slippery stones he struggled on until, dazed, drenched, and benumbed, he stumbled into a roughly circular opening amid the trees, where either by nature or design the brush had been cleared away for a radius of about fifty feet.

By the light afforded by the well-nigh incessant blaze of the lightning the place seemed strangely familiar to him, but the turmoil of external nature had so confused his mind that he could form no particular recollection of it save that its sight brought with it associations of fear, flight, and aversion. Then, with the suddenness and vividness of one of the flashes that illumined the spot, the tragedy that had been enacted upon it recurred to his mind. He saw Yéres rolling about in his death throes, saw him suddenly stiffen under his *misericordia* and, as another person, saw himself drag the body to the place where the Black Pine was to be erected. Instinctively his eyes followed the direction of his course in his mental vision. Yes, there it stood, the same great forest giant, but now, as he gazed, an indefinable feeling of awe mingled with dread seized upon him. The Pine seemed as if endowed with some unearthly personality, with something that was almost human, or a great deal more. To his mind, the great black mass of clustering boughs threateningly frowned down upon him so far below them. It alone of all its neighbors seemed to stand upright and immovable amid the surrounding confusion. Its tapering crest pointed heavenward in silent reproach, and to that heaven's tribunal the down-reaching branches, crooked and gnarled like fingers, beckoned him. Terrified, he turned to fly, but a sight still more terrible held him to the spot; simultaneous with the flash came the thunder burst, there was a deafening crack, a spiral of white fire ran down the Pine's trunk, shearing away the branches, whirling off the bark in clouds of scattering fuzz and lint, and, with a shower of spattering mud, plunged into the earth at its roots. Then, with a speechless terror, he saw that the mighty Pine, struck by lightning and propelled by the force of the wind, had begun to sway. Powerless to stir he watched it gradually moving; about its base the earth stirred and cracked open; slowly, slowly the forest monarch, ninety feet from base to crest, commenced to bend, and then, with ever-increasing impetus, inclined toward the earth. The gigantic shadow beetled, some sixty feet, directly over his head. He saw it coming, coming with a swiftness and with a force that fed itself upon each lessening second, yet he could not move hand, nor eye, nor foot. Ten feet away lay life and all its possibilities, yet he knew himself as certainly doomed as though the hemp were about his throat. All along the trunk ran a fierce snapping and rending noise, and now, as every fiber was strained to its uttermost limit of tension, collectively, like the tightly drawn cords of some huge viol, they gave forth a strident, high-keyed groan, the death cry of the falling Pine which, swelling by quick degrees to a wild, monotonous pitch, seemed to merge into almost a human intonation. Hark! where had he heard that cry before? A cry, long, shrill, piercing, and fraught with the accents of deadly suffering and despair. Where? Oh, dreadful thought, where but upon this very spot. The wild, unearthly sound that filled his ears was but the echo, long delayed, of that voice that fifteen years ago had rung unheeded and unheard through those same wooden solitudes. And even as he listened the blow fell. In an instant he was blinded, crushed, stunned, beaten down to the ground, and with Titanic force driven and dinted into the soil, while the roots of the avenging Pine, torn from their earthly bed, heaved themselves high into the air and, enfolded in their thousand, hand-like tentacles, shook aloft, as though in defiance of mortal precaution, the bleached and moldering bones of a clattering skeleton!

*   *   *

The next day the Sire de Taillebois, hunting the deer by royal permit, and led by the strange behavior of the pack, which, swerving from the trail of a wounded sounder, had brought up baying and excited about an open space in the forest, found the dead and the dying entangled in the roots and branches of the great Black Pine. The unknown skeleton was interred nearby, a cairn and a woodland shrine were shortly after erected over the spot, and the strange incident became one of the family legends of the Taillebois. The broken yet living body of Amelot, recognized by the Sire de Taillebois, was taken to the Manor. It was remarked by those who removed him from the tangled mass of broken and interlacing boughs that they exuded a thick and slimy sap, of a peculiar reddish tinge, unpleasant to the touch and particularly horrible to the sight.

Not many days after came woodcutters with ax and ox to the place where the Black Pine had fallen. "Pity," said they, "that so fine a tree should be left to rot to powder; trim its spreading branches, saw it into lengths and dispose of them to our no small modicum of profit at the next Marché de Roydeville, come next Candlemas."

And so the once great Pine, broken to piecemeal, found its devious ways to widely different corners of Europe—there to be devoted to widely different uses. Part, sawn into firm posts and stanchions and fenced with many a bolt and iron plate, went to build the gloomy portcullis at the prison of the Petit Châtelet of Paris. Part passed downward to sunny Cremona, where, carefully fashioned into delicately bowed sounding boards, polished, carven, and gaily painted, it was transformed into many a vielle, gittern, or quaintly droning linter-colo. While still another portion, traveling again to feudal Paris, was roughly hewn and squared into a tree whose roots were in law and justice, and which, watered by blood unlawfully spilled, bore an evil and a loathly fruit which men cared not to look upon.

Amelot had been one of those knights so rare as yet in the Twelfth Century, who, either dissatisfied with the scantiness of their annual rental or having actually lost all their feudal possessions, were obliged to live by the sale of their chivalry, whose valor and prowess were marketable articles to be haggled over and bargained for. To him war was a trade, tournaments, occasions where, not glory and honor, but material benefits, accruing from the sale of the forfeited arms and horses of vanquished knights, were to be won. He lived by his lance, he took life that he might live. Consequently when after many months of suffering and confinement he rose from the Sire de Taillebois's hospitable bed so maimed and shattered as never more to be able to sit a horse or couch a lance, he found his means of livelihood gone. Thus he had been obliged to have recourse to that nomadic vagabond existence, so romantic in the abstract, so bitter and degrading in the concrete reality, but which, taken altogether, has been of invaluable use to the librettists of the lighter Italian operas. He turned jongleur, what we today so erroneously call troubadour. His early education had in some degree fitted him for this profession, for it had been undertaken in the hall of the Baron of Taillebois, and chivalrous in its character had included something more than the rudiments of *la gaye science.* So he changed the lance for the lute, and carrying it under his arm went to that cradle of song and poetry where songsters were princes and princes songsters. He went to France, he went to Provence.

There was high revel in Château Sainte Edme.

The old Tourraine castle fluttered with bandelets and streamers from battlement to base. There had been tourneying in the outer court, hawking upon the *glacis,* archery and yeoman sports in the barbican, ring riding and lance practice in the plain just beyond the moat, tennis and *jeux de paume* in the *grande salle,* and, to crown all, a monster game of chess in which the pieces were the living men-at-arms of the Count of Sainte Edme, appareled and mounted as Knight, Bishop, and King and maneuvered by command of the contesting players stationed in the flanking towers of the south wall. And then, after the gigantic flash in the banquet hall, where the principal dishes were brought in to the sound of the trumpet by knights on horseback and in full caparison, the tables had been drawn and the jongleurs summoned to display their talents for the pleasure of the assembled company, stimulated by the prize of a perfect Arab, trapped in samite, which an esquire held at the farther end of the hall.

Amelot was one of the number of jongleurs present.

The Arab would bring 2,500 *livres Parisis* almost anywhere, and samite was worth 40 golden sous an ell.

He felt sure of success.

By virtue of that royal generosity, which even in the households of the lesser feudatories was exercised in the jongleurs' behalf, each one of the *amants de la gaye science* was offered the choice and made a present of the instrument with which he was to accompany his song. The methodical calculation of circumstance which his former life as mercenary had rendered so dominant in him was ever present with Amelot, and in consequence he had selected his song in reference to the character of those who were to listen to it. The majority of his audience spoke the liquid and sonorous *langue doc,* were dark, and of passionate, sensuous natures; with them love was a theme of never-failing interest; spirited war songs, ballads of the commonplace, or rondeaux and cantiliennes with their meaningless repetitions and complex construction were alike of little interest when compared to that passion which moved them so powerfully and which had made their *complaintes Pastoureaux* and *Bugerettes,* in which it was outpoured, so justly and so widely famous.

As songs of this character, with their slow movement and sustained notes, could best be rendered upon a vielle, Amelot chose such an instrument, of marvellous workmanship, and prepared to sing a *complainte* of very recent Italian composition.

But no sooner had he laid his bow to the quivering strings than a strange spirit, seemingly emanating from the richly carven sounding box, took possession of him; he was no longer master of himself, the bow refused to obey his will, driven by one stronger than his own. The vielle seemed on a sudden to be endowed with some strange inhuman life; its sleek, varnished surface glittered, aye, and seemed to swell and contract like the hide of a serpent, and, like a serpent's folds, the slack ends of the strings hanging from the pegs coiled themselves about his fingers and drove them along the keyboard with resistless force.

The vielle was playing of itself; by it he had become completely mastered, and had been transformed into the mere instrument of the instrument's self. But as the vielle played on and chord after chord was evolved, he felt the hair of his flesh to stand up with an unspeakable horror, *for the air was not his chosen composition,* but one that had been the favorite of Yéres, and that once heard he could never now forget by virtue of the associations of horror and remorse of a dreadful deed with which its falling rhythm was so nearly connected.

At length the slow, persistent monotone became unbearable; he felt that with its further continuance he should go insane, and though he was powerless to stop, he endeavored by a mighty effort to break into or jar upon it, anything to stop that low-pitched, crawling horror. Setting his teeth he drew the bow violently across the quivering strings with all the energy and power of his arm. Simultaneously the vielle responded, but with a chord, a sound, a cry that set his every nerve aprick with deadly horror, for the note evoked was the precise musical imitation of Yéres's death scream.

Then, with that sound, the spell was broken up. Panting as though from a death struggle Amelot sprang to himself once more, dashed the vielle to the ground, set his heel upon it, and trampled it into splinters, but even as he did so, the interior of the sounding board was exposed to view, and in its shattered fragments, sticky as they were with a revolting, thick, and darkly ruddy ichor, Amelot recognized the wood of the Black Pine of the Taillebois forest.

And now he looked about him, struggling to regain composure, wondering if it was his voice that but now had been so passionately speaking, and if it had been so, endeavoring, yet fearing, to recollect what he had said, or, dreadful thought, what he had confessed. But now, dispelling all doubt, the old Comte d'Edme rose from his chair and, since the counts of his name had always possessed magisterial rights upon their estate, said: "Sieur Amelot, it is my duty to inform you that all you have said will be used against you at the trial, which, since the crime you speak of was committed upon foreign soil, must be conducted at Paris. Sergeant-at-arms, remove the prisoner."

The trial was over.

The Echevins had pronounced the sentence. Through the throng the archers had forced a passage, and down the narrow Paris streets, down la Rue St. Honoré and la Rue St. Martin, over the island of La Cité Amelot had been conducted into the bowels of the Petit Châtelet, the guardian of the older city, battered by the then-recent attacks of the Northmen. Ancient as the days of Lutetia and the Roman occupation.

He was to be hanged upon the third day after that upon which the four walls of his cell had closed around him. These three days he had passed in bitter repentance over the folly of his confession, and in revolving with all his wonted care and discrimination the various possibilities of escape; but now was come the third day and as yet none such had afforded.

The air of the outside world was fresh in his face as they led him up into the *caille* of the Châtelet, and the noises that the earth made in its living were pleasant to his ears that for three nights had listened to the waters of the moat licking the green slime on the outside walls of his deep cell.

As he emerged into the *caille* or court, he beheld the mounted guard, which was to escort him to the Place Tratoir, drawn up in a hollow square. Some little delay had occurred, the provost's horse had slipped a shoulder, and Amelot and his escort were obliged to wait until another could be brought from the archer's barracks in the old Palais just across the river.

He became very watchful.

The gate of the fortress was up and the drawbridge down; outside he could catch a view of feudal Paris, gabioned and gabled, lying between its strips of blue Seine water and its strip of bluer sky. Straightest and longest of the streets of the medieval capital, la Rue St. Jacques lay open in a long vista directly in his line of vision; at the far end, la Porte St. Jacques; beyond it, the open fields and reach of green country; life, liberty, all for which men cared to live. He carefully approximated the distance that lay between him and the outer bank of the moat where the discarded horse of the provost was picketed. In his whilom vigor he could have covered it in a few bounds, the last of which would have set him astride of the horse, yet even now, with his feeble bones and cramped muscles, the end was worth the effort. He drew his swordless baldric tighter about his waist and looked about him. Close at his right hand a yeoman stood leaning upon his falchion, between him and the grate two others, one buckling on the plastron of the second; the usual guard at the portal paced back and forth the length of the narrow passage between the inner and outer gate, nursing his weapon. The warder of the prisons came to put the manacles upon him; Amelot held out his right wrist with his eyes intent upon the watch at the gate. He was slowly approaching that point in his walk where he would turn and with his back to the court recover the distance of his prescribed beat. The bracelet clicked as the warder locked it about Amelot's wrist. The watch was within a yard of the turning point; as slowly as possible Amelot extended his foot to be locked upon the chain which bound his hand, and as the warder bent to fetter it, the gate watch paused in his beat and listlessly turn about.

And then came a moment of excited shouting and a sudden outburst of confusion and rapid hurryings to and fro. Stepping upon the bending back of the warder Amelot had sprung over him. With two sweeping sidelong blows of his chain, swung as in his old-time knightly days he had swung the mace-at-arms, he had struck from his path the two yeomen who had attempted to bar it, and with every sinew stretched to its last limit of tension started toward the gate. The soldier on guard, warned by the cries in his rear, turned and saw him rushing down upon him. Too old in the service to interpose his body between liberty and the man who leaped toward it with such a face, he sprang into the guard-house and knocked away the catch from the windlass which lowered the grate; the path was clear. *Avi!* Amelot answered the shouts of his pursuers by another of triumph and defiance, which in chanting the terrible "Song of Roland" had so often fallen from his lips. There was nothing to stop him now, and he saw that, although the grate was beginning to stir, he would, if he could but maintain his present rate of speed, pass under it long before it fell, and at a flash he saw, too, what before had not occurred to him. The grate once fallen, and fallen behind him, would, with the loss of inestimable time, have to be again raised ere pursuit could be commenced.

Swift as an arrow he sprang forward toward the opening; laboriously, ponderously the huge portcullis momentarily narrowed it, yet he laughed aloud as he ran in the certainty of his triumph.

Hark!

It was not often that occasion rendered necessary the closing of the grate; the slots in which it ran were rusted thick with disuse, and now, as it slid through the reluctant grooves they uttered a shrill and grating remonstrance, as the heavy fabric of wood and iron dropped ever faster. The grating rose to a shrill scream. With that scream Amelot's laugh died upon his lips, and with a bound his heart sprang to his throat, and, like a choking lump, stuck there motionless; one with his heart, his limbs moved with it in answering accord, a single leap and they stiffened rigid—locked in horror. For the scream of the Châtelet's portcullis was the scream of the vielle of Château Edme, the scream of the falling Black Pine of the Taillebois forest; the eternal reverberation of the cry of the dying man, echo answering to echo, down all the lapse of fifteen years.

But the callous hardihood of the man, awed into abeyance for one moment, reasserted itself in another; he paused for an instant, gathered his shaking legs under him, and once more sprang forward with all the energy of despair.

Too late.

The few seconds he had lost sufficed to turn the trembling balance on the scale of desperate chance; simultaneous with his own onward bound, the portcullis, propelled by its own massive weight, gathering impetus from its every downward movement, with a hoarse rattle of chains and clanking iron and with a rasping, grinding streak of smoking grooves, fell.

Fell with a solid crash just as Amelot, with bowed shoulders, was bursting under its row of pointed teeth and, beneath it, as beneath some mighty guillotine, he was crushed to the pavement, bent double and venting low, quick screams.

Writhing in a spasm of pain beneath the fatal engine he tore and bit at it with nails and teeth, great splinters came away in his claw-like fingers, and within he recognized the wood of the Black Pine of Taillebois and saw his own blood mingling with its thick and ruddy sap.

But the end was not far now. The quivering body was heaped into a cart, and, at quick trot, hurried to the Place Tratoir.

The day had been very hot.

In the open squares of the city where the sunlight came flooding in like a palpable mass, hunting down and exterminating the timid, shrinking shadows, the heat was almost unbearable.

Altogether unbearable was it in this the Place Tratoir, packed to its uttermost with sweating and not-too-clean humanity, and many a white-lipped woman, aye, and men not a few, had been by officious friends extricated from the throng in a fainting and all but suffocating condition.

It was a superstitious age. Those nearest the newly erected gibbet, in the center of the square, often pointed to it and crossing themselves said: "What manner of man was this?" For the gibbet seemed very literally to be sweating blood. The heat had started the dormant sap from every pore, and in heavy resinous streams of dark-red hue it felt its way downward throughout the whole structure; at a little distance it looked like revolting blood.

The effect upon such a machine was horrible.

When, with the clatter of many hoofs and the jangling of many lances against the steel housing of those that carried them, the prisoner had arrived, such of the mob as had been near enough to note the condition of the gibbet saw him look upon it and then with a long shudder turn his eyes away, but the attendant priest, though he understood not their meaning, heard him mutter the words: "Again the Black Pine," and his head rolled forward upon the breast.

He was generally believed by those about him to have died, or at least to have lost consciousness, with this last word. But it was not so. To the last he retained every power of the mind, every sense of the body. He knew and felt when he was lifted out of the cart; he knew and felt when two archers supported him upon the platform; he knew and felt when the cord was adjusted about his neck; he knew and felt, with the recurrence of the old dread of the stormy night in the Taillebois forest, when the gibbet beetled over his head and when its shadow fell coldly across his brow, aye, and to the last he knew and felt, and even when the jar and wrench of the drop came, he knew and felt, and heard the timbers as they creaked and groaned beneath his weight give forth that dreadful cry which had tracked his own life to its close, ever since he had taken that of his fellow man in the shadowy forests of far-distant England, and that now, as its haunting accents filled the air about him, seem to thrill with ring of triumph and of final exultation.

It was the last sound he ever heard.

A DEFENSE OF THE FLAG

It had been the celebration of the feast of the Holy St. Patrick, and the various Irish societies of the city had turned out in great force—Sons of Erin, Fenians, Cork Rebels, and all. The procession had formed on one of the main avenues and had marched and countermarched up and down through the American city; had been reviewed by the mayor standing on the steps of the City Hall and wearing a green sash; and had finally disbanded in the afternoon in the business quarter of the city. So that now the streets in that vicinity were full of the perspiring members of the parade, the emerald color flashing in and out of the slow-moving maze of the crowd, like strands of green in the warp and woof of a loom.

There were marshals of the procession, with batons and big green rosettes, breathing easily once more after the long agony of sitting upon a nervous horse that walked sideways. There were the occupants of the endless line of carriages, with their green sashes, stretching their cramped and stiffened legs. There were the members of the various political clubs and secret societies, in their one good suit of ready-made clothes, cotton gloves, and silver-fringed scarfs. There was the little girl, with green tassels on her boots, who had walked by her father's side carrying a set bouquet of cut flowers in a lace paper-holder. There was the little boy who wore a green high hat, with a pipe stuck in the brim, and who carried the water for the band; and there were the members of the groups upon the floats, with overcoats and sacques thrown over their costumes and spangles.

The men were in great evidence in and around the corner saloons talking aloud, smoking, drinking, and spitting, and calling for "Jim," or "Connors," or "Duffy," over the heads of the crowd, and what with the speeches, and the beer, and the frequent fights, and the appropriate damning of England and the Orangemen, the day promised to end in right spirit and proper mood.

It so came about that young Shotover, on his way to his club, met with one of these groups near the City Hall, and noticed that they continually looked up toward its dome and seemed very well pleased with what they saw there. After he had passed them some little distance, Shotover, as well, looked up in that direction and saw that the Irish flag was flying from the staff above the cupola.

Shotover was American-bred and American-born, and his father and mother before him and their father and mother before them, and so on and back till one brought up in the hold of a ship called the *Mayflower*, further back than which it is not necessary to go.

He never voted. He did not know enough of the trend of national politics even to bet on the presidential elections. He did not know the names of the aldermen of his city, nor how many votes were controlled by the leaders of the Dirigo or Comanche Clubs; but when he was told that the Russian *moujik* or the Bulgarian serf, who had lived for six months in America (long enough for their votes to be worth three dollars), was as much of an American citizen as himself, he thought of the Shotovers who had framed the constitution in '75, had fought for it in '13 and '64, and wondered if this were so. He had a strange and stubborn conviction that whatever was American was right and whatever was right was American, and that somehow his country had nothing to be ashamed of in the past, nor afraid of in the future, for all the monstrous corruptions and abuses that obtained at present.

But just now this belief had been rudely jarred, and he walked on slowly to his club, the blood gradually flushing his face up to the roots of his hair. Once there, he sat for a long time in the big bay window, looking absently out into the street, with eyes that saw nothing, very thoughtful. All at once he took up his hat, clapped it upon his head with the air of a man who has made up his mind, and went out, turning in the direction of the City Hall.

When he arrived there, no one noticed him, for he made it a point to walk with a brisk, determined air, as though he were bent upon some especially important business, "which I am," he said to himself as he went on and up through tessellated corridors, between courtrooms and offices of clerks, commissioners, and collectors.

It was a long time before he found the right stairway, which was a circuitous, ladder-like flight that wormed its way upward between the two walls of the dome. The door leading to the stairway was in a kind of garret above the top floor of the building proper, and was sandwiched in between coal bunkers, water tanks, and gas meters. Shotover tried it, and found it locked. He swore softly to himself, and attempted to break it open. He soon concluded that this would make too much noise, and so turned about and descended to the floor below. A Negro, with an immense goiter and a black velvet skullcap, was cleaning the woodwork outside a county commissioner's door. He directed Shotover to the porter in the office of the Weather Bureau, if he wished to go up in the cupola for the view. It was after four by this time, and Shotover found the porter of the Weather Bureau piling the chairs on the tables and sweeping out after office hours.

"Well, you see," said this one, "we don't allow nobody to go up in the cupola. You can get a permit from the architect's office, but I guess they'll be shut up there by now."

"Oh, I'm sorry," said Shotover; "I'm leaving town tomorrow, and I particularly wanted to get the view from the cupola. They say you can see well out into the ocean."

The porter had ignored him by this time, and was sweeping up a great dust. Shotover waited a moment. "You don't think I could arrange to get up there this afternoon?" he went on. The porter did not turn around.

"We don't allow no one up there without a permit," he answered.

"I suppose," returned Shotover, "that you have the keys?"

No answer.

"You have the keys, haven't you—the keys to the door there at the foot of the stairs?"

"We don't allow no one to go up there without a permit. Didn't you hear me before?"

Shotover took a five-dollar gold piece from his pocket, laid it on the corner of a desk, and contemplated it with reflective sadness. "I'm sorry," he said; "I particularly wanted to see that view before I left."

"Well, you see," said the porter, straightening up, "there was a young feller jumped off there once, and a woman tried to do it a little while after, and the officers in the police station downstairs made us shut it up; but's long as you only want to see the view and don't want to jump off, I guess it'll be all right," and he leaned one hand against the edge of the desk and coughed slightly behind the other.

While he had been talking, Shotover had seen between the two windows on the opposite side of the room a very large wooden rack full of pigeonholes and compartments. The weather and signal flags were tucked away in these, but on the top was a great folded pile of bunting. It was sooty and grimy, and the new patches in it showed violently white and clean. But Shotover saw, with a strange and new catch at the heart, that it was tricolored.

"If you will come along with me now, sir," said the porter, "I'll open the door for you."

Shotover let him go out of the room first, then jumped to the other side of the room, snatched the flag down, and, hiding it as best he could, followed him out of the room. They went up the stairs together. If the porter saw anything, he was wise enough to keep quiet about it.

"I won't bother about waiting for you," said he, as he swung the door open. "Just lock the door when you come down, and leave the key with me at the office. If I ain't there, just give it to the fellow at the newsstand on the first floor, and I can get it in the morning."

"All right," answered Shotover, "I will," and he hugged the flag close to him, going up the narrow stairs two at a time.

After a long while he came out on the narrow railed balcony that ran around the lantern, and paused for breath as he looked around and below him. Then he turned quite giddy and sick for a moment and clutched desperately at the handrail, resisting a strong impulse to sit down and close his eyes.

Seemingly insecure as a bubble, the great dome rolled away from him on all sides down to the buttresses around the drum, and below that the gulf seemed endless, stretching down, down, down, to the thin yellow ribbon of the street. Underneath him, the City Hall itself dropped away, a confused heap of tinned roofs, domes, chimneys, and cornices, and beyond that lay the city itself spreading out like a great gray map. Over it there hung a greasy, sooty fog of a dark-brown color. In places the higher buildings overtopped the fog. Here, it was pierced by a slender church spire. In another place, a dome bulged up over it, or, again, some skyscraping office building shouldered itself above its level to the purer, cleaner air. Looking down at the men in the streets, Shotover could see only their feet moving back and forth underneath their hat brims as they walked. The noises of the city reached him in a subdued and steady murmur, and the strong wind that was blowing brought him the smell of the vegetable gardens in the suburbs, the odor of trees and hay from the more distant country, and occasionally a faint whiff of salt from the ocean.

The sight was a sort of inspiration to Shotover. The great American city, with its riches and resources, boiling with the life and energy of a new people, young, enthusiastic, ambitious, and so full of hope and promise for the future, all striving and struggling in the forepart of the march of empire, building a new nation, a new civilization, a new world, while over it all floated the Irish flag.

Shotover turned back, seized the halyards, and brought the green banner down with a single movement of his arm. Then he knotted the other bundle of bunting to the cords and ran it up. As it reached the top, the bundle twisted, turned on itself, unfolded, suddenly caught the wind, and then, in a single, long billow, rolled out into the stars and bars of Old Glory.

Shotover shut his teeth against a cheer, and the blood went tingling up and down through his body to his very fingertips. He looked up, leaning his hand against the mast, and felt it quiver and thrill as the great flag tugged at it. The sound of the halyards rattling and snapping came to his ears like music.

He was not ashamed then to be enthusiastic, and did not feel in the least melodramatic or absurd. He took off his hat, and, as the great flag blew out stiffer and snapped and strained in the wind, looked up at it and said over softly to himself: "Lexington, Valley Forge, Yorktown, Mexico, the Alamo, 1812, Gettysburg, Shiloh, the Wilderness."

Meanwhile the knot of people on the sidewalk below, that had watched his doings, had grown into a crowd. The green badge was upon every breast, and there came to his ears a sound that was out of chord with the minor drone, the worst sound in the human gamut, the sound of an angry mob.

The high, windy air and the excitement of the occasion began to tell on Shotover, so that when half an hour later there came a rush of many feet up the stairway, and a crash upon the door that led up to the lantern, he buttoned his coat tightly around him, and shut his teeth and fists.

When the door finally went down and the first man jumped in, Shotover hit him.

Terence Shannon told about this afterward. "It was a birdie. Ah, but say, y' ought to of seen um. He let go with his left, like de piston rod of de engine wot broke loose dat time at de power-house, an' Duffy's had an eye like a fried egg iver since."

The crowd paused, partly through surprise and partly because the body of Mr. Duffy lay across their feet and barred their way. There were about a dozen of them, all more or less drunk. The one exception was Terence Shannon, who was the candidate of the boss of his ward for a number on the force. In view of this fact, Shannon was trying to preserve order. He took advantage of the moment of hesitation to step in between Shotover and the crowd.

"Aw, say, youse fellows rattle me slats, sure. Do yer think the City Hall is the place to scrap, wid the jug only two floors below? Ye'll be havin' the whole shootin' match of the force up here in a minute. Maybe yer would like to sober up in the 'hole in the wall.' Now just pipe down quiet-like, an' swear um in reg'lar at the station house downstairs. Ye've got a straight disturbin'-the-peace case wid um. Ah, sure, straight goods. I ain't givin' yer no gee-hee."

But the crowd stood its ground and glared at Shotover over Shannon's head. Then Connors yelled and drew out his revolver. "B'yes, we've got a right," he exclaimed. "It's the boord av aldermen gave us the permit to show the green flag of ould Ireland here today. It's him as is breaking the law, not we, confound you." ("Confound you" was not what Mr. Connors said.)

"He's dead on," said Shannon, turning to Shotover. "It's all ye kin do. Yer're actin' agin the law."

Shotover did not answer, but breathed hard through his nose, wondering at the state of things that made it an offense against the American law to protect the American flag. But all at once Shannon passed him and drew his knife across the halyards, and the great flag collapsed and sank slowly down like a wounded eagle. The crowd cheered, and Shannon said in Shotover's ear: "'Twas to save yer life, me b'y. They're out for blood, sure."

"Now," said Connors, using several altogether impossible nouns and adjectives, "now run up the green flag of ould Ireland again, or ye'll be sorry," and he pointed his revolver at Shotover.

"Say," cried Shannon, in a low voice to Shotover—"say, he's dead stuck on doin' you dirt. I can't hold um. Aw, say, Connors, quit your foolin', will you; put up your flashbox—put it up, or—or——" But just here he broke off, and catching up the green flag, threw it out in front of Shotover, and cried, laughing, "Ye'll not have the heart to shoot now."

Shotover struck the flag to the ground, set his foot on it, and catching up Old Glory again, flung it round him and faced them, shouting:

"Now shoot!"

But at this, in genuine terror, Shannon flung his hat down and ran in front of Connors himself, fearfully excited, and crying out: "F'r Gawd's sake, Connors, you don't dast do it. Wake up, will yer, it's mornin'. Do yer want to hiv' us all jugged for twenty years? It's treason and rebellion, and I don't know *what* all, for every mug in the gang, if yer just so much as crook dat forefinger. Put it up, ye damned fool. This is a cat w'at has changed color."

Something of the gravity of the situation had forced its way through the clogged minds of the others, and, as Shannon spoke the last words, Connors's forearm was knocked up and he himself was pulled back into the crowd.

You cannot always foretell how one man is going to act, but it is easy to read the intentions of a crowd. Shotover saw a rush in the eyes of the circle that was contracting about him, and turned to face the danger and to fight for the flag as the Shotovers of the old days had so often done.

In the books, the young aristocrat invariably thrashes the clowns who set upon him. But somehow Shotover had no chance with his clowns at all. He hit out wildly into the air as they ran in, and tried to guard against the scores of fists. But their way of fighting was not that which he had learned at his athletic club.

They kicked him in the stomach, and, when they had knocked him down, stamped upon his face. It is hard to feel like a martyr and a hero when you can't draw your breath and when your mouth is full of blood and dust and broken teeth. Accordingly Shotover gave it up, and fainted away.

When the officers finally arrived, they made no distinction between the combatants, but locked them all up under the charge of "Drunk and Disorderly."

HIS SISTER

"Confound the luck," muttered young Strelitz in deep perplexity as he got up from the supper table and walked over to the mantelpiece, pulling at his lower lip as was his custom when thinking hard.

Young Strelitz lived in a cheap New York flat with his mother, to whose support he contributed by writing for the papers.

Just recently he had struck a vein of fiction that promised to be unusually successful. A series of short stories—mere sketches —which he had begun under the title "Dramas of the Curbstone," had "caught on," and his editor had promised to take as many more of them as he could write for the Sunday issue. Just now young Strelitz was perplexed because he had no idea for a new story. It was Wednesday evening already, and if his stuff was to go into the Sunday's paper it should be sent to the editor by the next day's noon at the latest.

"Blessed if I can dig up anything," he exclaimed as he leaned up against the mantelpiece, his forehead in a pucker.

He and his mother were just finishing their supper. Mrs. Strelitz brushed the crumbs from her lap and pushed back her chair, looking up at her son.

"I thought you were working on something this afternoon," she hazarded.

"It don't come out at all," he answered, as he drew a new box of cigarettes from his coat pocket. "It's that 'Condition of Servitude' stuff, and I can't make it sound natural."

"But that's a true story," exclaimed Mrs. Strelitz. "That really happened."

"That don't help matters any if it don't read like real life," he returned, as he opened the box of cigarettes. "It's not the things that have really happened that make good fiction, but the things that read as though they had."

"If I were you," said his mother, "I would try an experiment. You've been writing these 'Dramas of the Curbstone' without hardly stirring from the house. You've just been trying to imagine things that you think are likely to happen on the streets of a big city after dark, and you've been working that way so long that you've sort of used up your material—exhausted your imagination. Why don't you go right out—now—tonight, and keep your eyes open and watch what really happens, and see if you can't find something to make a story out of, or at least something that would suggest one. You're not listening, Conrad; what's the matter?"

It was true, young Strelitz was not listening. The box of cigarettes he had drawn from his pocket was a fresh one. While his mother was talking he had cut the green revenue stamp with his thumbnail, and had pushed open the box, had taken out a cigarette and had put it between his lips.

The box was one of those which contain, in addition to the cigarettes themselves, the miniature photograph of some bouffe actress, and Strelitz had found in his box one that was especially debonair. But as he looked at the face of the girl it represented he suddenly shifted his position and turned a little pale. He thrust the box back into his pocket, but closed his fist over the photograph as though to hide it. He did not light his cigarette.

"What's the matter, Conrad? You are not listening."

"Oh, yes I am," he answered. "I—nothing. I'm listening. Go on."

"Well, now, why don't you try that?"

"Try what?"

"Go out and look for a story on the streets."

"Oh, I don't know."

Without attracting his mother's attention, Strelitz looked again at the cigarette picture in his hand and then his glance went from it to a large crayon portrait that stood on a brass easel in the adjoining parlor. The crayon portrait was the head and bare shoulders of a young girl of seventeen or eighteen. The resemblance to Strelitz and his mother was unmistakable, but there was about the chin and the corners of the eyes a certain recklessness that neither of the others possessed. The mouth too was weak.

"You get right down to your reality then," continued Mrs. Strelitz. "Even if you do not find a story, you would find at least a background—a local color that you can observe much better than you can imagine."

"Yes, yes," answered Strelitz. He lounged out of the dining room, and going into the little parlor turned up the gas, and while his mother and the hired girl cleared away the table, fell to studying the two likenesses—the crayon portrait and the cigarette picture, comparing them with each other.

There was no room for doubt. The two pictures were of the same girl.

However, the name printed at the bottom of the cigarette picture was not that which young Strelitz expected to see.

"Violet Ormonde," he muttered, reading it. "That's the stage name she took. Poor Sabina, poor Sabina, to come to this." He looked again at the photograph of the bouffe actress, in her false bullfighter's costume, with its low-necked, close-fitting bodice, its tights, its high-laced kid shoes, its short Spanish cloak and foolish inadequate sword—a sword *opéra comique*. "Poor little girl," he continued under his breath as he looked at it, "she could have returned to us if she'd wanted to before she came to this. She could come back now. But where could one find her? What's become of her by this time?"

He was roused by the entrance of his mother and faced about, hastily thrusting the little photograph into his pocket and moving away from the crayon portrait on the brass easel, lest his mother should see him musing over it.

"Conrad," said Mrs. Strelitz, "you don't want to miss a week with your stories now that people have just begun to read them."

"I know," he admitted, "but what can I do? I haven't a single idea."

"Well, now, just do as I tell you. You try that. Go downtown and keep your eyes open and see if you can't see something you can make a story out of. Make the experiment, anyhow. You'll have the satisfaction of having tried. Why, just think, in a great city like this, with thousands and thousands of people, all with wholly different lives and with wholly different interests—interests that clash. Just think of the stories that are making by themselves every hour, every minute. There must be hundreds and hundreds of stories better than anything ever yet written only waiting for someone to take them down. Think of how near you may have come to an interesting story and never know it."

"That's a good saying, that last," observed young Strelitz, smiling in approval. "I'll make a note of that."

But his notebook was not about him, and rather than let his mother's remark slip his memory he jotted it down upon the back of the cigarette picture.

"Let's see, how does that go?" he said, writing. "'Think of how close one may come to an interesting story and never know it.' Well," added young Strelitz as he slipped the bit of cardboard back into his pocket. "I'll try your idea, but I haven't much faith in it. However, it won't do any hurt to get in touch with the real thing once in a while. I may get a suggestion or two."

"You may have an adventure or two," observed Mrs. Strelitz.

"Do the Haroun-al-Raschid act, hey?" answered her son. "Well, don't sit up for me," he went on, shrugging himself into his overcoat, "'cause if I get an idea I may go right up to the *Times* office and work it up in the reporters' room. Good night."

For more than two hours young Strelitz roamed idly from street to street. Now in the theater district, now in the slums and now in the Bowery. As a rule he avoided the aristocratic and formal neighborhoods, knowing by instinct that he would be more apt to find undisguised human nature along the poorer unconventional thoroughfares.

Hundreds of people jostled him, each with a hidden story no doubt; but all such as varied from the indistinguishable herd, resolved themselves into types, hackneyed overworked types, with nothing original about them. There was the Bowery boy; there was the tough girl; there was the young lady from the college settlement; there was the dude, the chippy, the bicycle girl, the tenement-house Irish woman, the bum, the drunk, the policeman, the Chinese laundry man, the coon in his plaid vest and the Italian vegetable man in his velvet jacket.

"I know you, I know you all," muttered young Strelitz, as one after another passed him. "I know you, and you, and you. There's

Chimmie Fadden, there's Cortlandt Van Bibber, there's Rags Raegen, there's George's Mother, there's Bedalia Herodsfoot, and Gervaise Coupeau and Eleanor Cuyler. I know you, every one; all the reading world knows you. You're done to death; you won't do, you won't do. Nothing new can be got out of you, unless one should take a new point of view, and that couldn't be done in a short story. Let's go into some of their saloons."

He entered several of the wine shops in the Italian quarter, but beyond the advertisement of a public picnic and games, where the second prize was a ton of coal, found nothing extraordinary.

"Now we'll try the parks," he said to himself. He turned about and started across town. As he went on the streets grew cleaner and gayer. The saloons became "elegant" bars. The dance halls, brilliantly lighted theaters. Here and there were cafes, with frosted-glass side doors, on which one read "Ladies' Entrance." Invariably there was a cabstand nearby.

"Ah, the Tenderloin," murmured Strelitz, slackening his pace. "I know you, too. I'll have a cocktail in passing, with you."

A large cafe, whose second story was gayly lighted, attracted him. He entered the bar on the ground floor and asked for a mild cocktail.

All at once he heard his name called. A party of men of his own age stood in the entrance of a little room that opened from the barroom, beckoning to him and laughing. Three of them he knew very well—Brunt of the *Times*, Jack Fremont, who had graduated with his class, and Angus McCloutsie, whom everyone called "Scrubby." The other men Strelitz knew to bow to. "Just the man we want," cried Jack Fremont as Strelitz came up.

"You're right in time," observed Scrubby, grinning and shaking his hand. "Come in, come in here with us." They pulled young Strelitz into the little room, and Brunt made them all sit down while he ordered beer.

"We're having the greatest kind of a time," Fremont began in an excited whisper. "All the crowd is upstairs—we got a room, we had supper—there's Dryden and Billy Libbey, and the two Spaulding boys and the 'Jay'—and all the old crowd. Y'ought to see Dick Spaulding sitting on the floor trying to put gloves on his feet; he says there were seven good reasons why he should not get full and that he's forgotten, every one. Oh, we're going to have the time of our lives tonight. You're just in time——"

"Joe's forgot the best part of it," broke in Scrubby. "There are three girls."

"Three girls?"

"Yes, sir, and one of them is the kind you read about. Just wait till you see her."

"I'm not going to wait," said young Strelitz. "I must go, right away. I'm working tonight." He finished his beer amongst their protests, and drew his handkerchief quickly out of his pocket and wiped his lips. But the others would not hear of his going.

"Oh, come along up," urged Brunt. "Just listen to that," cocking his head toward the ceiling, "and see what you're missing. That's Dick trying to remember." Strelitz hesitated. They certainly were having a glorious time up there—and the girls, too. He might at least go up and look in on them all. He began to reflect, pulling at his lower lip, his forehead in a pucker. If he went up there he would miss his story.

"No, no, I can't, fellows," he said decisively, rising from the table. "I've got to do some work tonight. Another time I'll join you; you have your good time without me this once." He pulled away from the retaining hands that would have held him, and ran out into the street, laughing over his shoulder at them, his hat on the back of his head.

"Well, if he's got to work, he's got to work," admitted Scrubby, as the swing doors flapped behind young Strelitz.

"He's going to miss the time of his life, though," put in Fremont. "Come on, let's go back to the crowd. What's that you got?"

"It's something that flipped out of Con's pocket, I think, as he pulled out his handkerchief. It's a cigarette picture."

"One of Con's fairies? Let's have a look."

They crowded together, looking over each other's shoulders. Suddenly there was an exclamation——

"Why, that's the girl that's upstairs now, the queen—the one that's so drunk. See the name; she said her name was Violet."

"Con must have known her."

"Too bad he had to shake the crowd."

"He would have had a great time with that girl."

"I say, what's he got written on the back?"

In the midst of a great silence, Brunt turned the cigarette picture to the light and read:

"Think how close one may come to an interesting story and never know it."

MAN PROPOSES

NO. I

It was at the seaside toward the end of the season. A cruiser had anchored just opposite the hotel, and there had been a ball on board. She and her mother had left early, and, of course, there was nothing left for him to do but to come home with them.

"If you want to very much," said her mother, as they reached the hotel veranda, "you can go back in the next launch, and come home later with your aunt, but I wouldn't stay much after eleven."

However, they didn't do this.

"I say," he exclaimed, as soon as they were alone, "you don't want to go back there, do you?—nothing but a lot of kid ensigns."

"Oh, I don't know," she replied indecisively, looking vaguely toward the cruiser's lights.

"Well, what's the matter with sitting out here on the porch a little while," he went on. "I don't think it will be cold, and there's a moon in about ten minutes."

They sat down together and talked in low tones about the "master of ceremonies of the hotel," who it was said had once been a monk in Lapland. Then the moon shrugged a red shoulder over the inky black line of the bathhouses.

"It *is* a little cold," she said. "Suppose we walk?"

There was a long boardwalk along the beach. It was here they found themselves in a few minutes. They walked slowly, he, bending a little forward, his hands thrust into his pockets, she, hatless, her hair a bit out of curl, her bare arms folded under her cape.

Rarely had he seen her in better spirits. They talked and laughed incessantly, and found huge amusement in trifles. For himself he was delightedly content. It was his hour, and he had her all to himself. There were no hectoring chaperons, no jingling pianos, no Other Fellows, no constrained and prolonged silences to mar his pleasure.

"It's a good thing I thought to wear my thick-soled shoes tonight," she exclaimed suddenly. "I shall catch it if they find out I didn't go back to the cruiser, but *I* don't care," she laughed. "But isn't this all so pretty?—the moon and the water and all—and so still. The noise of the breakers is just like part of the stillness, isn't it?—and, oh, *do* look back and see how pretty the ship looks from here."

It was pretty. The cruiser built itself up from the water as a huge, flat shadow, indistinct and strange against the gray blur of the sea and sky, looking now less like a ship of war than like an island-built fortress, turreted and curious. The lights from her ports glowed like a row of tiny footlights, while the faint clamor of the marine band, playing a Sousa quickstep, came to their ears across the water, small and delicately distinct, as if heard through a telephone.

All about them, seemingly coming from all quarters of the horizon at once, glowed the blue-white moonlight.

"Looks like a nickel-plated landscape," he remarked, looking toward the distant hills and promontories.

"Say *silver*, *do*," she answered, then suddenly interrupted herself, exclaiming, "Oh, I want to walk on the railroad track." They had come to that point where a disused siding of the railroad began to run parallel with the boardwalk. She stepped upon a rail and began to walk forward, swaying and balancing. All at once, and without knowing why, he put his arm around her waist, as if to steady her.

Then he choked down a gasp at his own temerity. It was astonishing to him how simply and naturally he had done the thing. It was as though he had done it in a dance. He had not premeditated it for a single instant, had not planned for it, had felt no hesitancy, no deliberation. Before he knew it, his arm was where it was, and the world and all things visible had turned a somersault.

In making the motion he had somehow thought to slide his arm beneath her cape, and the sensation of his hand and forearm against her firm, well-laced waist was, he thought, the most delightful thing he had ever experienced. He believed that this was the best moment of his life.

The question now was, would she let his arm remain where it was, or would she be angry and hurt? Had he gone too far, or did she care enough for him to allow such a liberty? Everything was happening in an instant of time. For a fraction of that instant he waited in a tremor of suspense. He felt that the next thing she should do or say would decide whether or not she was ever to care for him. One of two things, he told himself, must surely happen. Either she would resent what he had done, or plainly let him know that it was permissible.

It was a crisis.

But instead of acting as he expected, she suddenly seemed to concentrate all her thoughts on keeping her balance upon the rail. She did not pay the slightest attention to what he had done, but walked on, swaying and laughing as before. For a moment he was perplexed; then he saw his answer in her very silence. He instantly fell in with her mood, joyfully affecting ignorance of anything unusual. For a moment he debated the question of attempting to kiss her, but soon told himself that he had too much delicacy for that. This one great favor was enough at first.

"Really, we ought to be going home," she said, at length. "Just suppose *and* suppose if my aunt should come back from the cruiser, and Mama should find out I wasn't with her. I'd *more* than catch it."

They turned back and started home, but he kept his arm where it was, both of them still pretending to think of other things. Part of the way she walked on the rail again, and at one moment, losing her balance altogether, swayed toward him, and throwing out her hand instinctively, seized his shoulder furthest from her. On the instant he caught her wrist with his free hand and held her arm in place where it was.

At this she could no longer affect not to notice. She stopped suddenly and tried to pull away from him. Now it was *his* turn to assume a blissful ignorance; he looked at her surprised.

"Come along," he exclaimed. "I thought you said it was late; look there, the cruisers lights are out."

"Oh, but suppose somebody should *see* us," she gasped.

They did not talk much on the way back.

It was about quarter after twelve when they reached the hotel. The elevator had stopped running, the night clerk had just come on duty, and a porter was piling the office chairs together, making ready to sweep. She drank a glass of water at the ice cooler in the corner of the office and said she was going to bed. He went with her down the hall to her room, talking about a riding party the next day.

"I think I'll just see if Howard is in bed," she said, as she stopped before the door of the room that opened from her mother's and in which her little brother slept.

He followed her a couple of steps inside the room. Howard was there in bed, very warm and red, and sleeping audibly.

As she bent over the bed and smoothed out the pillows for her little brother, the sense of her beauty and her charm came over him again as keenly and vividly as when he had first met her. The hall was deserted, the hotel very quiet. He took a sudden resolution. He partially closed the door with his heel, and as she straightened up he put his arm about her neck and drew her head toward him. She turned to him then very sweetly, yielding with an infinite charm, and he kissed her twice.

Then he went out, softly closing the door behind him.

This was how he proposed to her. Not a word of what was greatest in their minds passed between them. But for all that they were no less sure of each other.

She rather preferred it that way.

NO. II

He was a coal heaver, and all that day he had been toiling at the dockyards with his fellows, carrying sacks of coal into a steamer's hold. The fatigue of work had been fearful; for full eight hours he had labored, wrestling with the inert, crushing weight of the sacks, fighting with the immense, stolid blocks of coal, smashing them with sledgehammers, sweating at his work, grimed like a Negro with the coal dust.

It was after six now, and he was on his way home. A fine, cold rain was falling, and over his head and shoulders he had thrown an empty coal sack, havelock-fashion.

He was an enormous man, strong as a dray horse, big-boned, heavily muscled, slow in his movements. His feet and hands were huge and knotted and twisted, and misshapen by hard usage. Through the grime of the coal dust one could but indistinctly make out his face. The eyes were small, the nose flat, and the lower jaw immense, protruding like the jaws of the carnivora, and thrusting the thick lower lip out beyond the upper. His father had been a coal heaver before him, and had worked at that trade until he had been killed in a strike. His mother had drunk herself into an asylum, and had died long ago.

He went on homeward through the fine drizzle. He thrust his hands into his trousers' pockets, gripping his sides with his elbows, drawing his shoulders together, shrinking into a small compass in order to be warm. His head was empty of all thought; his only idea was to get home and to be warm—to be fed, and then to sleep. At length he reached the house.

He pushed open the door of the kitchen, then paused on the threshold exclaiming, "What *you* doing here?"

She straightened up from the washtub and pushed the hair out of her eyes with the back of one smoking hand. "Yi sister's sick again, so I come in to bear a hand with the wash," she explained. "Yonder's your supper," and she jerked a bare elbow at the table with its linoleum cover. He did not answer, but went straight to his food, eating slowly with the delicious pleasure of a glutton, his huge jaws working deliberately, incessantly. She returned to the tubs, her shoulders rising and falling over the scrubbing board with a continuous rhythmical movement. There was no conversation.

He finished his supper and sat back in his chair with a long breath of satisfaction and content, and slowly wiped his lips with the side of his hand. Then he turned his huge body clumsily about and looked at her. Her back was toward him, but he could catch occasional indistinct glimpses of her face in the steam-blurred mirror that hung on the wall just above the tub.

She was not very young, and she was rather fat; her lips were thick and very red, and her eyes were small, her neck was large and thick and very white, and on the nape the hair grew low and curling.

Still watching her, he straightened out a leg, and thrusting his hand deep into his trousers' pocket drew out his short-stemmed clay pipe.

The tips of her bare elbows were red, and he noted with interest how this little red flush came and went as her arms bent and straightened.

In the other pocket he found his plug of tobacco and his huge horn-handled clasp knife. He settled his pipe comfortably in the corner of his mouth and began to cut off strips of tobacco from the plug with great deliberation.

As her body rose and fell, he watched curiously the wrinkles and folds forming and reforming about her thick corsetless waist.

He shut his knife with a snap and slipped it back into his pocket and began to grind the strips of tobacco between his palms, his eyes still fixed upon her.

Little beads of perspiration stood on her forehead and glistened in the hair on the nape of her neck. She breathed rapidly, and he remarked how her big white throat alternately swelled and contracted.

He took his pipe from his lips and filled it, stoppering it with his thumb, put it back unlighted between his teeth and dusted his leathery palms together slowly. Then he let his huge hands fall upon his knees, palms upward. He sat motionless, watching her fixedly. He was warm now, crammed with food, stupid, content, inert, and the animal within him purred and stretched itself. There was a long silence.

"Say," he exclaimed at length, with the brutal abruptness of crude, simple natures, "listen here. I like you better'n anyone else. What's the matter with us two gett'n' married, huh?"

She straightened up quickly and faced him, putting back her hair from her face with the same gesture of her soapy hand, drawing back from him frightened and bewildered.

"Say, will you?" he repeated. "Say, huh, will you? Come on, let's."

"No, no!" she exclaimed instinctively, refusing without knowing why, suddenly seized with the fear of him, the intuitive feminine fear of the male.

He could only say: "Ah, come on; ah, come on," repeating the same thing over and over again.

She, more and more frightened at his enormous hands, his huge square-cut head, and his enormous brute strength, cried out, "No, no!" shaking her head violently, holding out her hands and shrinking from him.

He laid his unlighted pipe on the table and got up and came near to her, his immense feet dragging and grinding on the bare floor.

"Ah, come on," he repeated; "what's the matter with us two gett'n married. Come on—why not?"

She retreated from him and stood on the other side of the tub.

"Why not?" he persisted. "Don't you like me well enough?"

"Yes."

"Then why not?"

"Because——"

"Ah, come on," he repeated. There was a silence, the hundred tiny bubbles in the suds of the washtub were settling and bursting with a prolonged and tiny crackling sound. He came around to where she stood, penning her into the corner of the room. "Huh, why not?" he asked. She was warm from her exertions at the tub, and as he stood over her she seemed to him to exhale a delicious feminine odor that appeared to come alike from her hair, her mouth, the nape of her neck. Suddenly he took her in his enormous arms, crushing down her struggle with his immense brute strength. Then she gave up all at once, glad to yield to him and to his superior force, willing to be conquered. She turned her head to him and they kissed each other full on the mouth, brutally, grossly.

NO. III

They had been out to the theater together and there was no chaperon. They knew each other well enough for that. On the front steps of her house she gave him her latchkey and he opened the front door for her. "You had better come in," she said, "and we'll find something to eat."

Every Monday evening they went to the theater and afterward had blue ribbon beer and pâté sandwiches in the kitchen of her house. It was a timeworn and time-honored custom of three months' standing, like his Thursday evening call and his meeting with her at the eleven o'clock service each Sunday.

She turned on the current in the hall and in the parlor, and went into the latter room and took off her things. He followed her about from place to place and listened attentively to her chaffing him because he had passed her on the street car the day before and had not seen her. He protested his innocence of any premeditated slight, and they went out into the kitchen both talking at the same time. It was all very gay, and they felt that they sufficed to themselves.

The Chinaman had set out the beer and sandwiches on the top of the ice chest in the laundry. She lighted every gas burner in sight and fetched the tray into the kitchen and got down the plates, while he opened the beer and filled the two glasses.

"There's pâté sandwiches," she said, punching each little pile with the tip of her finger as she spoke, "and sardine sandwiches and lettuce-an'-mayonnaise sandwiches, and don't say 'and the sand-which-is on the floor,' because you say it every time, and it's become an old joke that was funny once but isn't funny any more at all. Here, don't talk so much, but drink your beer. Here's success to you." They drank to each other, she sitting on the deal table, clicking her heels together; he, with his chair tilted back against the sink, grinning at her over the top of his glass.

"Huh!" he exclaimed all of a sudden, as he set down his glass and glanced about him, "four burners going full head in the kitchen at this hour. I won't let you do that when we're married, young woman, I can't afford it."

"When we're——" she shouted, adding furiously, "Well, I *do* like *that*."

"Yes, I thought you would," he replied calmly.

"You thought—you thought," she gasped, getting to her feet and gazing at him wide-eyed and breathless, "you were—you are—we are——"

"I am, thou art, he is," he interrupted, beginning to laugh, "which means that 'I am' quite determined to marry you, and 'thou art' to be my wedded wife, and 'he is,' that is to say your father, is to give us his consent and his blessing. I've been think-ing it all over, and I've made up my mind that it will be for next Thursday at twenty minutes after three."

"Oh, you have, have you!" she cried, breathing hard through her nose. "You might have asked *me* something about it."

"Oh, I didn't need to ask," he answered; "you see I'm pretty sure already."

"Pretty sure," she retorted. "Oh, this is fine. Oh, *isn't* this splendid! I just hate and loathe and detest and abhor and abomi-nate you."

"Yes, yes, I know," he answered, putting up his hand. "Does Thursday suit?"

"No, it *don't* suit," she flashed back at him. "It will be when I say and choose; I mean—I mean——"

He shouted with laughter, and her face blazed.

"I mean it won't *ever* be. Oh, I could—I could *bite* you."

"I think it will be Thursday," he said reflectively. "I'll call for you here in a carriage at twenty minutes after three, and in the meantime I'll see your father and fix things."

She sank into a chair and let her hands drop into her lap, palms upward, and drew a long breath or two, gazing at him helplessly and shaking her head.

"Well, of all the cool——"

"You see that will give us time enough for supper, and then we can take the eight fifty-five——"

"What are you talking about?" she inquired deliberately.

He went on unheeding:

"I got the tickets this afternoon."

"Tickets," she faltered.

"Um-hum," he answered, absently feeling in his inside pocket. "Here they are; see, this is the railroad ticket, and here's the Pullman ticket. Lower 10."

"Lower 10! It will be the *whole section*. I—I mean, of course—I—you. *Oh—h*, how I hate you!"

"That will give us two days in New York. I wired for a state-room day before yesterday. It's the *St. Paul*. She sails on the twenty-third. Do you like the boat?"

"Oh, go right on, go right on!" she cried, waving her hands at him. "Don't mind *me*."

"Well, that's as far ahead as I've planned now. I don't think we would want to stay over on the other side more than four months. Then, you know, there's the expense."

She was about to answer when they both heard the front door close. "That's Dave," she exclaimed. Her brother came out into the kitchen in evening dress.

"Hello, hello," he said. "Beer and skittles, domestic enough; can I belong? Beer's flat, of course, but I'll have a skittle, if you don't mind," and he began to eat a sandwich, telling them the whiles where he had been and what he had been doing.

He and the brother fell a-talking. She sat silent, very thoughtful, looking at him from time to time.

"Well," said he, at last, "I must be going," adding, as he turned to her, "I've a deal to do in the next few days." She made a little gasp, and got up and went with him into the front hall, leaving the brother to grumble over the flatness of the beer. She helped him on with his overcoat. There was a silence. He stood with his hand on the knob of the door. "Good night," she said, adding, as she always did, "When am I to see you again?"

"Well," he answered, suddenly grave, very much in earnest, "when *are* you to see me again? It's up to you, little girl; what's your answer? Now, when shall I come?"

She didn't answer at once. In the stillness they heard the humming of the cable in the street outside. Then there was an opening and closing of doors as the brother came out of the kitchen.

"Quick," he said, putting a hand on her shoulder, he'll be here in a minute. When am I to see you again?"

Then she turned to him:

"Oh, I suppose Thursday, at twenty minutes after three."

NO. IV

"Going away!" she echoed, suddenly facing him and looking at him with wide eyes.

"That's right," he admitted.

They were sitting on the green bench, all carved and whittled, that stood at the end of the pier. Behind them, on the shore, the lights of the huge hotel were winking out one by one. It was rather late.

"Yes," he went on, looking vaguely about on the floor of the pier. "The governor wired me two or three days ago, but I didn't want to say anything about it and spoil our fun. You see, the governor is starting a branch agency in Liverpool, and he wants me to go over there and take charge. I suppose I shall have to—well, have to locate there—live there—permanently. The governor knows a lot of people there. Then there's the business. You see, I've been in the firm now for nearly ten years—ever since I graduated—and I know the details pretty well—better than a new man—and the governor's business methods. That new lamp for the submarine torpedo boats is a pet hobby of his. I improved a self-adjuster to regulate the pressure that tickled him almost to death. He thinks I can get the contract for lighting all the new torpedo boats that the——"

"Oh, what do I care about all that?" she burst out, suddenly. "How about *me?*"

"How about you?" he repeated, pretending not to understand. "How—what do you mean about you?"

There was a silence. Then:

"Haven't you got anything more than that to say to me?" she asked bravely, sitting up very straight and trying to catch his eye.

"Well, what can I say?" he answered, smiling at her. "We've had an awfully good time here, little girl, and I shall never forget you. You don't know how sorry I am to leave you. You must promise to write to me, won't you?—just 'care of the office,' you know."

"But you—you don't seem to understand," she began.

"Send me a letter on board ship," he went on, quickly—"she sails a week from Saturday—just to wish me *bon voyage.* It's mighty good, you know, to get a letter when you are leaving for a long voyage like that. Oh, I say, little girl, don't do that. Look here; for heaven's sake don't take it to heart like that. Look here, look at me. I didn't know that you—that you really cared."

"Of course you know," she cried, looking at him from over her crumpled handkerchief. "How could you have thought anything else? I *told* you, didn't I? I made it plain enough, and you told me that you cared," she flashed out, "again and again—you know what you made me think—what you gave me to understand, and I—and—oh, what is going to become of me now!"

Suddenly she slid both her arms around his neck and turned her face close to his, as loving, as yielding, and yet as absolutely irresistible as when he had first known her. She was wonderfully pretty. He felt that he was weakening. There was something in him, some sensual second-self, that the girl evoked at moments such as this; something that was of the animal and would not be gainsaid. He saw her in a false light, knowing that it was a false light, yet willing to be deceived, finding a certain abnormal pleasure in the trickery. The odor of the cheap little sachets and toilet water that she used, mingled with the delicate feminine smell of her hair and neck, was delicious to him.

"Well, now, that will be all right, little girl," he said, taking her face in both his hands.

"How do you mean all right?" she demanded. "You *told* me that you loved me."

"Well, I *do* love you."

"As much as ever?"

He hesitated.

"Yes; as much as ever."

"Say it after me, then." She was so pretty and so pitiful as she looked at him through her tears, and he was so sorry for her, so loath to hurt her, that he said, half meaning the words:

"I love you."

"More than anyone else?"

"More than anyone else."

"Say it all together," she insisted.

"Well, then, I love you more than anyone else."

"And so——" she prompted.

"And so what?" he answered, fencing.

"And so you will—will. Oh, don't make me do it *all*. When two people love each other more than anyone else, then what?"

He hesitated again. After all, she was very pretty, and she loved him, and he loved her—that is, he—— But he had gone too far now. And, after all, why not?

"Little girl," he said suddenly, "I think you'll have to marry me."

"Do you mean it—*really?*" she demanded.

He laughed a note, willing even then to draw back.

"Guess I do or I wouldn't say it."

"You wouldn't dare say that to my mother."

"I'm afraid I wouldn't take that dare."

"Well, then," she said suddenly, rising to her feet. "I *dare* you to say so right now. We'll go up to the hotel right away."

He was in for it now, and so rose with her, saying:

"Come along, then."

They went up to the hotel and found her mother and father sitting on the porch in front of their rooms.

"Come inside, Ma," she said, as they came up; "I want to speak to you."

He followed the girl and her mother into the little parlor of their suite. She turned to him:

"Now," she said, "say it now, just what you said to me." He smiled a bit, embarrassed. The girl stood to one side, glancing from one to the other. Then he spoke:

"This little girl says she loves—me—and I—and—well—we think—we want—we want to be married."

"Well, dear—me—suz," exclaimed her mother, and sat down with a gasp. She got up again immediately, calling: "Popper, for the land's sakes just come in here and listen to all this." Her father entered in his shirtsleeves. "If these two children haven't gone an' got engaged," continued her mother. "Now, what have you got to say to that?"

"I got no kick comin'," admitted the old man; "guess we know the young fellar well enough."

"Kick! no, of course, we've got no kick," answered his wife.

"But we don't want any five-year-engagement business about it; sooner the better. Guess that'll suit you," she added, turning to him.

"The sooner the better," he admitted, with a smile.

"Well, now, look here," said her mother. "My mouth is just as dry as a pocket; you go down to the bar and have 'em send up a couple of quart bottles of beer, and come up here and we'll talk this thing over."

He went out, and started down the porch in the direction of the bar. On the steps that led down into the garden, he paused and looked at his watch, wondering if the barroom would be open as late as this.

Inside the case of his watch was pasted the photograph of the head of a girl. It was not the picture of the girl he had just left. Holding the watch in his hand turned to the moonlight, he looked at it a long time, very thoughtful.

"I wonder——" he muttered to himself at length. Then he shut the watch with a snap. "What kind of a mess have I got into now?" he said.

NO. V

Immediately after the collision that night the stranger had backed off, and by the time that the party on board the yacht had pulled themselves together and had begun to look about them after the first blind rush of terror, her lights had disappeared. It was not possible that the steamer which had run them down had sunk. She was no doubt a tramp cattle-boat, steel-built, huge, well able to take care of herself. She had struck Trefethan's little thousand-ton yacht a glancing blow under the bilge, and then sheered off into the night as silently and as mysteriously as she had come up. What made matters worse was that the great hawk-beaked clipper bow of the tramp had smashed into the *Viking's* only seaworthy boat. All this had happened some eighteen hours since. During that time the party aboard the *Viking* had regarded their situation from three distinct and different points of view. First had come the panic, that blind, deaf fear of something terrible and unknown. Then as the day whitened and drew toward noon, and that menacing list to port grew no worse, a feeling of relief and ultimate safety began to spread among them, and Trefethan's skipper, who had been down in the hold with the carpenter all the morning, came on deck at last and smiled at them and shook hands with Trefethan.

And then after luncheon, with the wind shifting and coming in vast puffs out of the west and north, and the sea building up higher and higher over the port rail, the vague trouble and the sense of disaster returned and persisted, and they began to remember the smashed boat. This time, however, there was no panic. But there was something in the air, something in the very look of the yacht, and the feel of the rolling deck, and the queer laboring of the bows as she strained to right herself after each roll to port, that did not seem to need explanation. Then came the slow, cold clutch at the heart that tightened and persisted in spite of all effort at deception, first bewilderment, then an instant's return of the unreasoning terror of the previous night, a moment's hysterical protest against the inevitable, and last of all a certain grim calmness, an abandoning of all hope. The men and women aboard that pleasure yacht sinking in mid-ocean turned about and faced, as best they might, the Death that reached upward toward them from the crest of every oncoming wave. The skipper had told them at last that it was but a matter of hours. If the sea went down with the sun, they might keep up until the next morning.

They two were under the lee of the wheel house. Some of the women were below in the cabin where Mrs. Trefethan was trying to read the services. Trefethan himself and the skipper were forward setting out rockets and roman candles against the coming of the night. She held on to the nickel handrail of the house and looked vaguely out across the empty waste of tumbling green water, her hair whipping across her face. He stood close to her, sometimes watching her, and sometimes fixing his eyes upon the distress signal, with its ominous reversed flag that was flying from the peak. For a long time neither had spoken. Then at last:

"I suppose—this is the end," she said.

"I suppose so," he answered.

"What *should* one do?" she went on, looking at him. "There is a best way to meet it but I *can't* think. It's all so confused. Death— this kind is—is so huge and so very terrible that *anything*—yes, anything—one poor human being can do or say seems so pitiful, so inadequate. The last thing one does in life should be—at least, one wants it to be—a thing that is generous, noble, or kind. It may be a false idea, but one has that feeling just the same, and instead of being noble or kind I can only feel bewildered and stunned and confused."

He was looking at her, but he was hardly listening.

"It *is* the end of everything," he said. "That is why I want you to try and listen to what I am going to say. I know I could not choose a worse opportunity, but the power of choosing is beyond us now. Please listen. Nothing matters now, but—do I really need to tell you? Haven't you understood? Haven't you seen all the time how it was with me? How much I loved you? Do you know— it seems a poor thing to say—but if I thought that you cared—that you cared for me—in that way, I wouldn't mind about this business, if we were together and cared. What did I come with

Trefethan for? You know it was just to be with you. I love you. Yes, I know it all sounds lame and poor, but I love you, and if things—if this had not happened, I would have asked you to be my wife. Of course, nothing matters now, but when I saw that there was no chance for the yacht I felt that I must let you know. No, not that either, for I am sure you know already, but I felt that I must be sure of you, must know your answer. Tell me. Suppose all had gone well, that we had got in safe, and I had asked you. You can tell me now. What difference does anything make now? What would you have said?"

While he spoke, she had been trying to think rapidly. She knew what he was going to say, had been long expecting it. Even before she had sailed, Jack had joked her about this man, declaring that he was "The Other Fellow." Jack had even wished their engagement should be announced before she had left him for that long summer's cruise. But she had told him—what he knew already—that he was sure of her, that it could be easily put off until she got back. To reassure him, she had even promised that she would marry him within a month of her return. Dear old Jack, he had not been out of her thoughts once during all the dreadful tension of those last eighteen hours.

But now this man, this "Other Fellow," who waited there for her answer upon this doomed wreck. What was she to say to him? She liked him, there was no doubt of that. After Jack there was no one else she cared for more. Two days ago she could have had the heart to tell him the bitter truth, almost as hard for her to utter as for him to hear. She had resolutely made up her mind to tell him that she did not care for him as soon as he should speak. There was a long silence.

"I know," he said, at length, "that I take an unfair advantage of you at such a moment as this. But it is quite impossible for me to tell you how much it would mean for me even in the short time that is left."

Never in all her life had she felt more pity and sorrow than she did for him at this moment. He was so fine and strong and virile, and she liked him so much in every other way. For her it was veritable anguish to hurt him in this the last moment of his life. In any other circumstances it would have been different.

At once an idea occurred to her. In the confused distorted condition of her mind it seemed as if she had arrived at a solution. Why not tell him that which he wanted to hear, even if she did not mean it? What difference would it make if they were all to die there within the next few hours? Would not this be the kind, noble deed that she had spoken about? Why not, if it would make him happier? Did anything matter now? There was little time to reflect.

"Tell me," he insisted, "do you care? Would you have been my wife?" She did not answer at once, but put out her hand and laid it upon his as it was gripped whitely over the nickel handrail of the house. He caught it up suddenly in both his own.

"And you mean——" he exclaimed.

"If it would make you any happier to know," she answered, "yes, I *do* care."

He put his arm about her neck and she let him kiss her on the cheek, all wet and cold with the flying spray.

Trefethan and the skipper came running down the deck together with one of the sailors.

The sailor swung himself to the shrouds and ran aloft. Then he paused, sweeping the horizon with a telescope.

"What do you make her out?" shouted the skipper.

"She's truck down yet, sir," answered the sailor, "but I think she's a French liner. She's heading towards us by the way the smoke builds."

JUDY'S SERVICE OF GOLD PLATE

She was a native of Guatemala, and so, of course, was said to be Mexican, and she lived in the alley by the county jail, three or four doors above the tamale factory. Her trade was something odd. The Chinamen, who go down to the sea in ships from San Francisco to Cape St. Lucas, off the coast of Lower California, and fish for sharks there, used to bring the livers of these sharks back to her. She would boil the oil out of these livers and turn over the product to a redheaded Polish Jew named Knubel, who bottled it and sold it to San Francisco as cod-liver oil. Knubel made money in the business. She was his only employee. Her name, incidentally, was Lambala Largomarsini, which was no doubt the reason why she was called "Judy."

Knubel lived on Telegraph Hill, on the ledge of the big cliff there, and used to lie awake on windy nights waiting for his house to be blown off that ledge. Knubel had always lived on Telegraph Hill. When he was forty he had had a stroke of paralysis, and had lost the use of his left leg. The result of this stroke was that Knubel was held a prisoner on the Hill. He dared not go down into the city below him, because he knew he could never get back. How could he, stop and think? No horse ever gets to the top of the Hill. The cable cars and electric cars turn their headlights upon the Hill and shake their heads and go around in the valley by Stockton Street. The climb is bad enough for a man with two healthy legs, but for a paralytic—— Knubel was trapped upon the Hill, trapped and held prisoner. He never saw Kearny or Montgomery or Market Street after his stroke. He never saw the new *Call* building, or the dome upon the City Hall but from afar, and the Emporium was to him but a distant granite cliff. In the newspaper, he who lived in San Francisco read about what was happening there as you and I and all the rest of us read about what is happening in London or in Paris or in Vienna, and this with the roar of that San Francisco actually in his ears, like the bourdon of a tremendous organ.

Judy of course was wretchedly poor, for the salary that Knubel allowed her for boiling down the shark's livers would not have fattened a self-respecting chessy cat. Knubel himself was a horrible old miser; he had made a little fortune in cod-liver oil, but he kept it tied up in three old socks in a starch box underneath the floor of his cellar. He had a passion for gold, and turned all his silver and greenbacks into gold as fast as he could. He lived in a room about as big as a trunk, at back of an Italian wine shop where there was a "Bocce" court, and Judy used to come and see him here once a month and get her salary and make her report.

One day when Judy had come to get her orders and her money from Knubel she found him bending his red head over his table testing an old brass collar button with nitric acid.

"I found him bei der stairs on der bottom," he explained to Judy. "Berhaps he is of gold. Hey, yes?"

Judy looked at the collar button.

"That ain't gold," she declared. "Huh! you can't fool me on gold. I seen more gold in my day than you've seen tin, Mister Knubel."

Knubel's eyes were gimlets on the instant.

"Vat you say?"

"When I was a kid in Guatemala my folks had a set of gold plate, dishes you know, hundreds of 'em, all solid gold."

Here we touch on Judy's one mania. She believed and often stated that at one time her parents in Guatemala were enormously wealthy, and in particular were possessed of a wonderful service of gold plate. She would describe this gold plate over and over again to anyone who would listen. Why there were more than a hundred pieces, all solid red gold. Why there were goblets and punch bowls and platters and wine pitchers and ladles, why the punch bowl itself was worth a fortune. Ignorant enough on other subjects, and illiterate enough, Heaven knows, once started on her gold plate, Judy became almost eloquent. Of course, no one believed her story, and rightly so because the gold plate never did exist. How Judy got the idea into her mind it was impossible to say, but it was the custom of people who knew of her mania to set her going and watch her while she rocked to and fro with closed eyes, and hands clasped over her knee, chanting monotonously, "More'n a hundred pieces, and all red, red gold," and so on and so on.

For a long while her hearers scoffed; then at last she suddenly made a convert; old Knubel, the redheaded Polish Jew, believed her story on the instant. As often as Judy would come to make her monthly report on the shark liver industry, old Knubel would start her going, swallowing her words as a bullion bag swallows coin. As soon as Judy had finished he would begin to ask her questions.

"The gold voss soft, hey? und ven you rapped him mit der knuckles now, he rung out, didn't he, yes?"

"Sweeter'n church bells."

"Ah, sweeter nor der church bells, shoost soh. I know, *I* know. Now let's have ut egain, more'n a hoondurt bieces. Let's haf ut all *eg*-gain." And again and again Judy would tell him her wonderful story, delighted that she had at last found a believer. She would chant to Knubel by the hour, rocking herself back and forth, her hands clasped on her knee, her eyes closed. Then by and by Knubel, as he listened to her, caught *himself* rocking back and forth, keeping time with her.

Then Knubel found excuses for Judy's coming to see him oftener than once a month. The manufacture of cod-liver oil out of sharks' livers needed a great deal of talking over. Knubel knew her story by heart in a few weeks and began to talk along with her. There in that wretched room over the "Bocce" court on the top of Telegraph Hill, the "Mexican" hybrid woman and the Polish Jew, redheaded and paralytic, rocked themselves back and forth with closed eyes and clasped hands singsonging, "More'n a hundred pieces, all red, red gold"—"More den a hoondurt bieces und alle rad gold."

It was a strange sight to see.

"Judy," said Knubel, one day when the woman was getting ready to leave, "vy you go, my girl, eh? Stay hier bei me, und alle-ways you will me dat story getellen, night und morgen, alle-ways. Hey? Yes?"

So it came about that the two were—we will say married, and for over a year night und morgen Judy the story of the wonderful gold plate ge-told. Then a little child was born to her. The child has nothing to do here; besides it died right away; no doubt its little body wasn't strong enough to hold in itself the blood of the Hebrew, the Spaniard and the Slav. It died. At the time of its birth Judy was out of her head, and continued so for upwards of two weeks. Then she came to herself and was as before.

Not quite. "Now ve vill have ut once eg-gain," said Knubel, "pe-gin, more dan one hoondurt bieces, und alle rad, rad gold."

"What's you talkin's about?" said Judy with a stare.

"Vy, about dat gold blate."

"I don't know about any gold plate, you must be crazy, Knubel. I don't know what you mean."

Nor did she. The trouble of her mind at the time of her little child's birth had cleared her muddy wits of all hallucinations. She remembered nothing of her wonderful story. But now it was Knubel whose red head was turned. Now it was Knubel who went about telling his friends of the wonderful gold service. But his mania was worse than Judy's.

"You've got ut, you've got ut zum-vairs, you she-swine," he would yell, clubbing Judy with a table leg. "Vair is ut? You've hidun ut. I know you've got ut. Vair is dose bunch powl, vair is dose tsoop sboon?"

"How do I know?" Judy would shout, dodging his blows.

In fact how *did* she know?

Knubel went from bad to worse, ransacked the house, pulled up the flooring, followed Judy when she went out as well as his game leg would allow, and peeped at her through keyholes when she was at home.

Knubel and Judy had a neighbor who was also an acquaintance, a Canadian woman who did their washing. Judy was sitting before the kitchen stove one morning when this woman came after the weekly wash. She was dead and must have been dead since the day before, for she was already cold. The Canadian woman touched her shoulder, and Judy's head rolled sideways and showed where Knubel had—well, she was dead.

Late in the day the officers found Knubel hiding about the old abandoned Pavilion that stands on top of the Hill. When arrested he had a sack with him full of rusty tin pans, plates and old tomato cans that he had gathered from the dump heaps.

"I got ut," said Knubel to himself, "I got ut, more dan a hoondurt pieces. I got ut at last."

The manufacture of cod-liver oil from shark livers has languished of late, because of the hanging of Mister Knubel at San Quentin penitentiary.

And all this, if you please, because of a service of gold plate that never existed.

SHORTY STACK, PUGILIST

Over at the Big Dipper Mine a chuck tender named Kelly had been in error as regards a box of dynamite sticks, and Iowa Hill had elected to give an "entertainment" for the benefit of his family.

The program, as announced upon the posters that were stuck up in the post office and on the door of the Odd Fellows' Hall, was quite an affair. The Iowa Hill orchestra would perform, the livery-stable keeper would play the overture to *William Tell* upon his harmonica, and the town doctor would read a paper on "Tuberculosis in Cattle." The evening was to close with a "grand ball."

Then it was discovered that a professional pugilist from the Bay was over in Forest Hill, and someone suggested that a match could be made between him and Shorty Stack "to enliven the entertainment." Shorty Stack was a bedrock cleaner at the Big Dipper, and handy with his fists. It was his boast that no man of his weight (Shorty fought at a hundred and forty) in Placer County could stand up to him for ten rounds, and Shorty had always made good this boast. Shorty knew two punches, and no more—a short-arm jab under the ribs with his right, and a left uppercut on the point of the chin.

The pugilist's name was McCleaverty. He was an out-and-out dub—one of the kind who appear in four-round exhibition bouts to keep the audience amused while the "event of the evening" is preparing—but he had had ring experience, and his name had been in the sporting paragraphs of the San Francisco papers. The dub was a welterweight and a professional, but he accepted the challenge of Shorty Stack's backers and covered their bet of fifty dollars that he could not "stop" Shorty in four rounds.

And so it came about that extra posters were affixed to the door of the Odd Fellows' Hall and the walls of the post office to the effect that Shorty Stack, the champion of Placer County, and Buck McCleaverty, the Pride of Colusa, would appear in a genteel boxing exhibition at the entertainment given for the benefit, etc., etc.

Shorty had two weeks in which to train. The nature of his work in the mine had kept his muscles hard enough, so his training was largely a matter of dieting and boxing an imaginary foe with a rock in each fist. He was so vigorous in his exercise and in the matter of what he ate and drank that the day before the entertainment he had got himself down to a razor edge, and was in a fair way of going fine. When a man gets into too good condition, the least little slip will spoil him. Shorty knew this well enough, and told himself in consequence that he must be very careful.

The night before the entertainment Shorty went to call on Miss Starbird. Miss Starbird was one of the cooks at the mine. She was a very pretty girl, just turned twenty, and lived with her folks in a cabin near the superintendent's office, on the road from the mine to Iowa Hill. Her father was a shift boss in the mine, and her mother did the washing for the "office." Shorty was recognized by the mine as her "young man." She was going to the entertainment with her people, and promised Shorty the first "walk around" in the "Grand Ball" that was to follow immediately after the Genteel Glove Contest.

Shorty came into the Starbird cabin on that particular night, his hair neatly plastered in a beautiful curve over his left temple, and his pants outside of his boots as a mark of esteem. He wore no collar, but he had encased himself in a boiled shirt, which could mean nothing else but mute and passionate love, and moreover, as a crowning tribute, he refrained from spitting.

"How do you feel, Shorty?" asked Miss Starbird.

Shorty had always sedulously read the interviews with pugilists that appeared in the San Francisco papers immediately before their fights and knew how to answer.

"I feel fit to fight the fight of my life," he alliterated proudly. "I've trained faithfully and I mean to win."

"It ain't a regular prize fight, is it, Shorty?" she inquired. "Pa said he wouldn't take Ma an' me if it was. All the women folk in the camp are going, an' I never heard of women at a fight, it ain't genteel."

"Well, I d'n know," answered Shorty, swallowing his saliva. "The committee that got the program up called it a genteel boxing exhibition so's to get the women folks to stay. I call it a four-round go with a decision."

"My, itull be exciting!" exclaimed Miss Starbird. "I ain't never seen anything like it. Oh, Shorty, d'ye think you'll win?"

"I don't *think* nothun about it. I *know* I will," returned Shorty defiantly. "If I once get in my left uppercut on him, *huh!*" and he snorted magnificently.

Shorty stayed and talked to Miss Starbird until ten o'clock, then he rose to go.

"I gotta get to bed," he said. "I'm in training, you see."

"Oh, wait a minute," said Miss Starbird, "I been making some potato salad for the private dining of the office, you better have some; it's the best I ever made."

"No, no," said Shorty stoutly, "I don't want any."

"Hoh," sniffed Miss Starbird airily, "you don't need to have any."

"Well, don't you see," said Shorty, "I'm in training. I don't dare eat any of that kinda stuff."

"Stuff!" exclaimed Miss Starbird, her chin in the air. "No one *else* ever called my cooking stuff."

"Well, don't you see, don't you see?"

"No, I don't see. I guess you must be 'fraid of getting whipped if you're so 'fraid of a little salad."

"What!" exclaimed Shorty indignantly. "Why, I could come into the ring from a jag and whip him; 'fraid! *Who's* afraid? I'll show you if I'm afraid. Let's have your potato salad, an' some beer, too. Huh! *I'll* show you if I'm afraid."

But Miss Starbird would not immediately consent to be appeased.

"No, you called it stuff," she said, "an' the superintendent said I was the best cook in Placer County."

But at last, as a great favor to Shorty, she relented and brought the potato salad from the kitchen and two bottles of beer.

*   *   *

When the town doctor had finished his paper on "Tuberculosis in Cattle," the chairman of the entertainment committee ducked under the ropes of the ring and announced that: "The next would be the event of the evening and would the gentlemen please stop smoking." He went on to explain that the ladies present might remain without fear and without reproach as the participants in the contest would appear in gymnasium tights, and would box with gloves and not with bare knuckles.

"Well, don't they always fight with gloves?" called a voice from the rear of the house. But the chairman ignored the interruption.

The "entertainment" was held in the Odd Fellows' Hall. Shorty's seconds prepared him for the fight in a back room of the saloon, on the other side of the street, and toward ten o'clock one of the committeemen came running in to say:

"What's the matter? Hurry up, you fellows, McCleaverty's in the ring already, and the crowd's beginning to stamp."

Shorty rose and slipped into an overcoat.

"All ready," he said.

"Now mind, Shorty," said Billy Hicks, as he gathered up the sponges, fans, and towels, "don't mix things with him. You don't have to knock him out, all you want's the decision."

Next, Shorty was aware that he was sitting in a corner of the ring with his back against the ropes, and that diagonally opposite was a huge red man with a shaven head. There was a noisy, murmuring crowd somewhere below him, and there was a glare of kerosene lights over his head.

"Buck McCleaverty, the Pride of Colusa," announced the master of ceremonies, standing in the middle of the ring, one hand under the dub's elbow. There was a ripple of applause. Then the master of ceremonies came over to Shorty's corner, and, taking him by the arm, conducted him into the middle of the ring.

"Shorty Stack, the Champion of Placer County." The house roared; Shorty ducked and grinned and returned to his corner. He was nervous, excited. He had not imagined it would be exactly like this. There was a strangeness about it all; an unfamiliarity that made him uneasy.

"Take it slow," said Billy Hicks, kneading the gloves, so as to work the padding away from the knuckles. The gloves were laced on Shorty's hands.

"Up you go," said Billy Hicks, again. "No, not the fight yet, shake hands first. Don't get rattled."

Then ensued a vague interval, that seemed to Shorty interminable. He had a notion that he shook hands with McCleaverty, and that someone asked him if he would agree to hit with one arm free in the breakaway. He remembered a glare of lights, a dim vision of rows of waiting faces, a great murmuring noise, and he had a momentary glimpse of someone he believed to be the referee, a young man in shirtsleeves and turned-up trousers. Then everybody seemed to be getting out of the ring and away from him, even Billy Hicks left him after saying something he did not understand. Only the referee, McCleaverty, and himself were left inside the ropes.

"Time!"

Somebody, that seemed to Shorty strangely like himself, stepped briskly out into the middle of the ring, his left arm before him, his right fist clinched over his breast. The crowd, the glaring lights, the murmuring noise, all faded away. There only remained the creaking of rubber soles over the resin of the boards of the ring and the sight of McCleaverty's shifting, twinkling eyes and his round, close-cropped head.

"Break!"

The referee stepped between the two men and Shorty realized that the two had clinched, and that his right forearm had been across McCleaverty's throat, his left clasping him about the shoulders.

What! Were they fighting already? This was the first round, of course, somebody was shouting.

"That's the stuff, Shorty."

All at once Shorty saw the flash of a red-muscled arm, he threw forward his shoulder ducking his head behind it, the arm slid over the raised shoulder and a bare and unprotected flank turned toward him.

"Now," thought Shorty. His arm shortened and leaped forward. There was a sudden impact. The shock of it jarred Shorty himself, and he heard McCleaverty grunt. There came a roar from the house.

"Give it to him, Shorty."

Shorty pushed his man from him, the heel of his glove upon his face. He was no longer nervous. The lights didn't bother him.

"I'll knock him out yet," he muttered to himself.

They fiddled and feinted about the ring, watching each other's eyes. Shorty held his right ready. He told himself he would jab McCleaverty again on the same spot when next he gave him an opening.

"*Break!*"

They must have clinched again, but Shorty was not conscious of it. A sharp pain in his upper lip made him angry. His right shot forward again, struck home, and while the crowd roared and the lights began to swim again, he knew that he was rushing McCleaverty back, back, back, his arms shooting out and in like piston rods, now for an uppercut with his left on the——

"*Time!*"

Billy Hicks was talking excitedly. The crowd still roared. His lips pained. Someone was spurting water over him, one of his seconds worked the fans like a windmill. He wondered what Miss Starbird thought of him now.

"*Time!*"

He barely had a chance to duck, almost double, while McCleaverty's right swished over his head. The dub was swinging for a knockout already. The round would be hot and fast.

"Stay with um, Shorty."

"That's the stuff, Shorty."

He must be setting the pace, the house plainly told him that. He stepped in again and cut loose with both fists.

"*Break!*"

Shorty had not clinched. Was it possible that McCleaverty was clinching "to avoid punishment"? Shorty tried again, stepping in close, his right arm crooked and ready.

"*Break!*"

The dub was clinching. There could be no doubt of that. Shorty gathered himself together and rushed in, uppercutting viciously; he felt McCleaverty giving way before him.

"He's got um going."

There was exhilaration in the shout. Shorty swung right and left, his fist struck something that hurt him. Sure, he thought, that must have been a good one. He recovered, throwing out his left before him. Where was the dub? not down there on one knee in a corner of the ring? The house was a pandemonium, near at hand someone was counting, "one—two—three—four——"

Billy Hicks shouted, "Come back to your corner. When he's up go right in to finish him. He ain't knocked out yet. He's just taking his full time. Swing for his chin again, you got him going. If you can put him out, Shorty, we'll take you to San Francisco."

"Seven—eight—nine——"

McCleaverty was up again. Shorty rushed in. Something caught him a fearful jar in the pit of the stomach. He was sick in an instant, racked with nausea. The lights began to dance.

"*Time!*"

There was water on his face and body again, deliciously cool. The fan windmills swung round and round. "What's the matter, what's the matter?" Billy Hicks was asking anxiously.

Something was wrong. There was a lead-like weight in Shorty's stomach; a taste of potato salad came to his mouth; he was sick almost to vomiting.

"He caught you a hard one in the wind just before the gong, did he?" said Billy Hicks. "There's fight in him yet. He's got a straight-arm body blow you want to look out for. Don't let up on him. Keep——"

"*Time!*"

Shorty came up bravely. In his stomach there was a pain that made it torture to stand erect. Nevertheless, he rushed, lashing out right and left. He was dizzy; before he knew it he was beating the air. Suddenly his chin jolted backward, and the lights began to spin; he was tiring rapidly, too, and with every second his arms grew heavier and heavier and his knees began to tremble more and more. McCleaverty gave him no rest. Shorty tried to clinch, but the dub sidestepped, and came in twice with a hard right and left over the heart. Shorty's gloves seemed made of iron; he found time to mutter, "If I only hadn't eaten that stuff last night."

What with the nausea and the pain, he was hard put to it to keep from groaning. It was the dub who was rushing now; Shorty felt he could not support the weight of his own arms another instant. What was that on his face that was warm and tickled? He knew that he had just strength enough left for one more good blow; if he could only uppercut squarely on McCleaverty's chin it might suffice.

"*Break!*"

The referee thrust himself between them, but instantly McCleaverty closed again. Would the round *never* end? The dub swung again, missed, and Shorty saw his chance; he stepped in, uppercutting with all the strength he could summon up. The lights swam again, and the roar of the crowd dwindled to a couple of voices. He smelt whisky.

"Gimme that sponge." It was Billy Hicks voice. "He'll do all right now."

Shorty suddenly realized that he was lying on his back. In another second he would be counted out. He raised himself, but his hands touched a bed quilt and not the resined floor of the ring. He looked around him and saw that he was in the back room of the saloon where he had dressed. The fight was over.

"Did I win?" he asked, getting on his feet.

"Win!" exclaimed Billy Hicks. "You were knocked out. He put you out after you had him beaten. Oh, you're a peach of a fighter, you are!"

Half an hour later when he had dressed, Shorty went over to the Hall. His lip was badly swollen and his chin had a funny shape, but otherwise he was fairly presentable. The Iowa Hill orchestra had just struck into the march for the walk around. He pushed through the crowd of men around the door looking for Miss Starbird. Just after he had passed he heard a remark and the laugh that followed it:

"Quitter, oh, what a quitter!"

Shorty turned fiercely about and would have answered, but just at that moment he caught sight of Miss Starbird. She had just joined the promenade or the walk around with some other man. He went up to her:

"Didn't you promise to have this walk around with me?" he said aggrievedly.

"Well, did you think I was going to wait all night for you?" returned Miss Starbird.

As she turned from him and joined the march Shorty's eye fell upon her partner.

It was McCleaverty.

THE THIRD CIRCLE

There are more things in San Francisco's Chinatown than are dreamed of in Heaven and earth. In reality there are three parts of Chinatown—the part the guides show you, the part the guides don't show you, and the part that no one ever hears of. It is with the latter part that this story has to do. There are a good many stories that might be written about this third circle of Chinatown, but believe me, they never will be written—at any rate not until the "town" has been, as it were, drained off from the city, as one might drain a noisome swamp, and we shall be able to see the strange, dreadful life that wallows down there in the lowest ooze of the place—wallows and grovels there in the mud and in the dark. If you don't think this is true, ask some of the Chinese detectives (the regular squad are not to be relied on), ask them to tell you the story of the Lee On Ting affair, or ask them what was done to old Wong Sam, who thought he could break up the trade in slave girls, or why Mr. Clarence Lowney (he was a clergyman from Minnesota who believed in direct methods) is now a "dangerous" inmate of the State Asylum—ask them to tell you why Matsokura, the Japanese dentist, went back to his home lacking a face—ask them to tell you why the murderers of Little Pete will never be found, and ask them to tell you about the little slave girl, Sing Yee, or—no, on the second thought, don't ask for that story.

The tale I am to tell you now began some twenty years ago in a See Yup restaurant on Waverly Place—long since torn down—where it will end I do not know. I think it is still going on. It began when young Hillegas and Miss Ten Eyck (they were from the East, and engaged to be married) found their way into the restaurant of the Seventy Moons, late in the evening of a day in March. (It was the year after the downfall of Kearney and the discomfiture of the sandlotters.)

"What a dear, quaint, curious old place!" exclaimed Miss Ten Eyck.

She sat down on an ebony stool with its marble seat, and let her gloved hands fall into her lap, looking about her at the huge hanging lanterns, the gilded carven screens, the lacquer work, the inlay work, the colored glass, the dwarf oak trees growing in satsuma pots, the marquetry, the painted matting, the incense jars of brass, high as a man's head, and all the grotesque gimcrackery of the Orient. The restaurant was deserted at that hour. Young Hillegas pulled up a stool opposite her and leaned his elbows on the table, pushing back his hat and fumbling for a cigarette.

"Might just as well be in China itself," he commented.

"Might?" she retorted; "we are in China, Tom—a little bit of China dug out and transplanted here. Fancy all America and the Nineteenth Century just around the corner! Look! You can even see the Palace Hotel from the window. See out yonder, over the roof of that temple—the Ming Yen, isn't it?—and I can actually make out Aunt Harriett's rooms."

"I say, Harry (Miss Ten Eyck's first name was Harriett), let's have some tea."

"Tom, you're a genius! Won't it be fun! Of course we must have some tea. What a lark! And you can smoke if you want to."

"This is the way one ought to see places," said Hillegas, as he lit a cigarette; "just nose around by yourself and discover things. Now, the guides never brought us here."

"No, they never did. I wonder why. Why, we just found it out by ourselves. It's ours, isn't it, Tom, dear, by right of discovery?"

At that moment Hillegas was sure that Miss Ten Eyck was quite the most beautiful girl he ever remembered to have seen. There was a daintiness about her—a certain chic trimness in her smart tailor-made gown, and the least perceptible tilt of her crisp hat that gave her the last charm. Pretty she certainly was—the fresh, vigorous, healthful prettiness only seen in certain types of unmixed American stock. All at once Hillegas reached across the table, and, taking her hand, kissed the little crumpled round of flesh that showed where her glove buttoned.

The China boy appeared to take their order, and while waiting for their tea, dried almonds, candied fruit, and watermelon rinds, the pair wandered out upon the overhanging balcony and looked down into the darkening streets.

"There's that fortune-teller again," observed Hillegas presently. "See—down there on the steps of the joss house?"

"Where? Oh, yes, I see."

"Let's have him up. Shall we? We'll have him tell our fortunes while we're waiting."

Hillegas called and beckoned, and at last got the fellow up into the restaurant.

"Hoh! You're no Chinaman," said he, as the fortune-teller came into the circle of the lantern light. The other showed his brown teeth.

"Part Chinaman, part Kanaka."

"Kanaka?"

"All same Honolulu. Sabe? Mother Kanaka lady—washum clothes for sailor peoples down Kaui way," and he laughed as though it were a huge joke.

"Well, say, Jim," said Hillegas; "we want you to tell our fortunes. You sabe? Tell the lady's fortune. Who she going to marry, for instance."

"No fortune—tattoo."

"Tattoo?"

"Um. All same tattoo—three, four, seven, plenty lil birds on lady's arm. Hey? You want tattoo?"

He drew a tattooing needle from his sleeve and motioned toward Miss Ten Eyck's arm.

"Tattoo my arm? What an idea! But wouldn't it be funny, Tom? Aunt Hattie's sister came back from Honolulu with the prettiest little butterfly tattooed on her finger. I've half a mind to try. And it would be so awfully queer and original."

"Let him do it on your finger, then. You never could wear evening dress if it was on your arm."

"Of course. He can tattoo something as though it was a ring, and my marquise can hide it."

The Kanaka-Chinaman drew a tiny fantastic-looking butterfly on a bit of paper with a blue pencil, licked the drawing a couple of times, and wrapped it about Miss Ten Eyck's little finger—the little finger of her left hand. The removal of the wet paper left an imprint of the drawing. Then he mixed his ink in a small sea shell, dipped his needle, and in ten minutes had finished the tattooing of a grotesque little insect, as much butterfly as anything else.

"There," said Hillegas, when the work was done and the fortune-teller gone his way; "there you are, and it will never come out. It won't do for you now to plan a little burglary, or forge a little check, or slay a little baby for the coral round its neck, 'cause you can always be identified by that butterfly upon the little finger of your left hand."

"I'm almost sorry now I had it done. Won't it ever come out? Pshaw! Anyhow I think it's very chic," said Harriett Ten Eyck.

"I say, though!" exclaimed Hillegas, jumping up; "where's our tea and cakes and things? It's getting late. We can't wait here all evening. I'll go out and jolly that chap along."

The Chinaman to whom he had given the order was not to be found on that floor of the restaurant. Hillegas descended the stairs to the kitchen. The place seemed empty of life. On the ground floor, however, where tea and raw silk were sold, Hillegas found a Chinaman figuring up accounts by means of little balls that slid to and fro upon rods. The Chinaman was a very gorgeous-looking chap in round horn spectacles and a costume that looked like a man's nightgown, of quilted blue satin.

"I say, John," said Hillegas to this one, "I want some tea. You sabe?—upstairs—restaurant. Give China boy order—he no come. Get plenty much move on. Hey?"

The merchant turned and looked at Hillegas over his spectacles.

"Ah," he said calmly, "I regret that you have been detained. You will, no doubt, be attended to presently. You are a stranger in Chinatown?"

"Ahem!—well, yes—I—we are."

"Without doubt—without doubt!" murmured the other.

"I suppose you are the proprietor?" ventured Hillegas.

"I? Oh, no! My agents have a silk house here. I believe they sublet the upper floors to the See Yups. By the way, we have just received a consignment of India silk shawls you may be pleased to see."

He spread a pile upon the counter, and selected one that was particularly beautiful.

"Permit me," he remarked gravely, "to offer you this as a present to your good lady."

Hillegas's interest in this extraordinary Oriental was aroused. Here was a side of the Chinese life he had not seen, nor even suspected. He stayed for some little while talking to this man, whose bearing might have been that of Cicero before the Senate assembled, and left him with the understanding to call upon him the next day at the Consulate. He returned to the restaurant to find Miss Ten Eyck gone. He never saw her again. No white man ever did.

There is a certain friend of mine in San Francisco who calls himself Manning. He is a Plaza bum—that is, he sleeps all day in the old Plaza (that shoal where so much human jetsam has been stranded), and during the night follows his own devices in Chinatown, one block above. Manning was at one time a deep-sea pearl diver in Oahu, and, having burst his ear drums in the business, can now blow smoke out of either ear. This accomplishment first endeared him to me, and latterly I found out that he knew more of Chinatown than is meet and right for a man to know. The other day I found Manning in the shade of the Stevenson ship, just rousing from the effects of a jag on undiluted gin, and told him, or rather recalled to him the story of Harriett Ten Eyck.

"I remember," he said, resting on an elbow and chewing grass. "It made a big noise at the time, but nothing ever came of it—nothing except a long row and the cutting down of one of Mr. Hillegas's Chinese detectives in Gambler's Alley. The See Yups brought a chap over from Peking just to do the business."

"Hachet man?" said I.

"No," answered Manning, spitting green; "he was a two-knife Kai Gingh."

"As how?"

"Two knives—one in each hand—cross your arms and then draw 'em together, right and left, scissor-fashion—damn near slashed his man in two. He got five thousand for it. After that the detectives said they couldn't find much of a clue."

"And Miss Ten Eyck was not so much as heard from again?"

"No," answered Manning, biting his fingernails. "They took

her to China, I guess, or maybe up to Oregon. That sort of thing was new twenty years ago, and that's why they raised such a row, I suppose. But there are plenty of women living with Chinamen now, and nobody thinks anything about it, and they are Canton Chinamen, too—lowest kind of coolies. There's one of them up in St. Louis Place, just back of the Chinese theater, and she's a Sheeny. There's a queer team for you—the Hebrew and the Mongolian—and they've got a kid with red, crinkly hair, who's a rubber in a Hammam bath. Yes, it's a queer team, and there's three more white women in a slave-girl joint under Ah Yee's tan room. There's where I get my opium. They can talk a little English even yet. Funny thing—one of 'em's dumb, but if you get her drunk enough she'll talk a little English to you. It's a fact! I've seen 'em do it with her often—actually get her so drunk that she can talk. Tell you what," added Manning, struggling to his feet, "I'm going up there now to get some dope. You can come along, and we'll get Sadie (Sadie's her name), we'll get Sadie full, and ask her if she ever heard about Miss Ten Eyck. They do a big business," said Manning, as we went along. "There's Ah Yee and these three women and a policeman named Yank. They get all the yen shee—that's the cleanings of the opium pipes, you know, and make it into pills and smuggle it into the cons over at San Quentin prison by means of the trusties. Why, they'll make five dollars' worth of dope sell for thirty by the time it gets into the yard over at the Pen. When I was over there, I saw a chap knifed behind a jute mill for a pill as big as a pea. Ah Yee gets the stuff, the three women roll it into pills, and the policeman, Yank, gets it over to the trusties somehow. Ah Yee is independent rich by now, and the policeman's got a bank account."

"And the women?"

"Lord! they're slaves—Ah Yee's slaves! They get the swift kick most generally."

Manning and I found Sadie and her two companions four floors underneath the tan room, sitting cross-legged in a room about as big as a big trunk. I was sure they were Chinese women at first, until my eyes got accustomed to the darkness of the place. They were dressed in Chinese fashion, but I noted soon that their hair was brown and the bridge of each one's nose was high. They were rolling pills from a jar of yen shee that stood in the middle of the floor, their fingers twinkling with a rapidity that was somehow horrible to see.

Manning spoke to them briefly in Chinese while he lit a pipe, and two of them answered with the true Canton singsong—all vowels and no consonants.

"That one's Sadie," said Manning, pointing to the third one, who remained silent the while. I turned to her. She was smoking a cigar, and from time to time spat through her teeth man-fashion. She was a dreadful-looking beast of a woman, wrinkled like a shriveled apple, her teeth quite black from nicotine, her hands bony and prehensile, like a hawk's claws—but a white woman beyond all doubt. At first Sadie refused to drink, but the smell of Manning's can of gin removed her objections, and in half an hour she was hopelessly loquacious. What effect the alcohol had upon the paralyzed organs of her speech I cannot say. Sober, she was tongue-tied—drunk, she could emit a series of faint bird-like twitterings that sounded like a voice heard from the bottom of a well.

"Sadie," said Manning, blowing smoke out of his ears, "what makes you live with Chinamen? You're a white girl. You got people somewhere. Why don't you get back to them?"

Sadie shook her head.

"Like um China boy better," she said, in a voice so faint we had to stoop to listen. "Ah Yee's pretty good to us—plenty to eat, plenty to smoke, and as much yen shee as we can stand. Oh, I don't complain."

"You know you can get out of this whenever you want. Why don't you make a run for it someday when you're out? Cut for the Mission House on Sacramento Street—they'll be good to you there."

"Oh!" said Sadie listlessly, rolling a pill between her stained palms, "I been here so long I guess I'm kind of used to it. I've about got out of white people's ways by now. They wouldn't let me have my yen shee and my cigar, and that's about all I want nowadays. You can't eat yen shee long and care for much else, you know. Pass that gin along, will you? I'm going to faint in a minute."

"Wait a minute," said I, my hand on Manning's arm. "How long have you been living with Chinamen, Sadie?"

"Oh, I don't know. All my life, I guess. I can't remember back very far—only spots here and there. Where's that gin you promised me?"

"Only in spots?" said I; "here a little and there a little—is that it? Can you remember how you came to take up with this kind of life?"

"Sometimes I can and sometimes I can't," answered Sadie. Suddenly her head rolled upon her shoulder, her eyes closing. Manning shook her roughly.

"Let be! let be!" she exclaimed, rousing up; "I'm dead sleepy. Can't you see?"

"Wake up, and keep awake, if you can," said Manning; "this gentleman wants to ask you something."

"Ah Yee bought her from a sailor on a junk in the Pei Ho River," put in one of the other women.

"How about that, Sadie?" I asked. "Were you ever on a junk in a China river? Hey? Try and think."

"I don't know," she said. "Sometimes I think I was. There's lots of things I can't explain, but it's because I can't remember far enough back."

"Did you ever hear of a girl named Ten Eyck—Harriett Ten Eyck—who was stolen by Chinamen here in San Francisco a long time ago?"

There was a long silence. Sadie looked straight before her, wide-eyed; the other women rolled pills industriously; Manning looked over my shoulder at the scene, still blowing smoke through his ears; then Sadie's eyes began to close and her head to loll sideways.

"My cigar's gone out," she muttered. "You said you'd have gin for me. Ten Eyck! Ten Eyck! No, I don't remember anybody named that." Her voice failed her suddenly, then she whispered:

"Say, how did I get that on me?"

She thrust out her left hand, and I saw a butterfly tattooed on the little finger.

BULDY JONES, *CHEF DE CLAQUE*

I

The first time I saw Juliana was in the gardens of the *Palais Royale*, while the band of the *Garde Nationale* was playing a potpourri of *La Favorita*, the work to be performed that same evening at the Grand Opera House.

"Pipe her off!" says Horse Wilson. "Quick! There she goes with Buldy Jones. Mind your eye. That's her—Juliana."

"Juliana?"

"'Member about her?"

As I was still a *nouveau* in the *atelier* Julien, I had not yet learned the traditions and legends of the place, so the Horse explained. (He was a colonial Englishman from Australia, a man with no education, but a wonderful colorist.)

"Oh, I s'y," he observed. "Not know about Juliana! W'y, you *are* jolly green. Well, here's the how of it. She's an orphan-born, so you might s'y. Just turned up fit as how-do-you-do on the steps of the *atelier*—Julien's, y' know—one morning, sucking her thumb, kicking up her heels."

"Kicking——"

"H'ut! you bounder. She was a young 'un—a byeby."

"Oh, a foundling, then?"

"Aye, and the students at Julien's adopted her; called her Juliana. And ever since they have supported her. Once a month the hat goes 'round. Strike me straight, Julien's has been food an' drink, an' gran'dad an' brother an' sister an' forbears to Juliana."

"Does she pose?"

"Not in the public *ateliers*. Only to a few chaps. To Buldy Jones, of course, an' to Bismarck an' Bayard, an' once she posed to me. I did my *hors de concours* from her. Of course, we're in love with her—Bismarck an' Bayard an' me. That goes without s'yin'. But she only loves Buldy."

"Does she paint?"

"Lord love you, no. Man, she *sings*, like a bally nightingyle. She'll be on the styge soon. *Would* go now, but we're sitting tight, so as to make her debut more of a whoop-an'-bang affair. We're backin' her, y' see. Buldy Jones an' me an' Bayard an' Bismarck. Buldy, he puts up the lucre. He's got oodles of it. And we others— well, we sort of fetch-an'-carry like. We got Bertrand—y' know of him, the big *impresario*—to take her up, an' he an' Buldy air wire- workin' an' bell-hangin' an' spring-pushin' to get her on some- where. We can make the Châtelet with *La Dame Blanche* without harf tryin'; but Bertrand an' Buldy want better'n that for the young 'un. He's fair dotty about her—Bertrand."

And just here the God-from-the-machine, Buldy Jones, came up. He was—it is possible the affair may be remembered—the big American who fought the baseball duel with Camme.* He was enormously wealthy, and a college-trained athlete, but preferred the painting of miniature Louis Quinze pictures (and he six feet two in his boots!) to private yachts or the coaching of football elevens at home in America.

"Say," he began excitedly as soon as he was within speaking radius—"say, have you heard? We've pulled it off. Bertrand got a letter from the director last night. Juliana has just told me."

"I s'y, ol' chap," began the Horse, "*don't* tell us it's a go."

"That's *what!*" declared Buldy Jones.

"Strike! in what?"

"*Van Arteveldt*—the page's part."

"Oh, nifty, where?"

"Well, Horse Wilson, where do you guess?"

"The Châtelet."

"Another shot."

"Opéra Comique."

"Clean miss, m' son."

"The Renaissance."

"No score."

"Buldy, it ain't, it *ain't* the Grand Opera House?"

*Refers to an incident in "This Animal of a Buldy Jones."

"*Bull's-eye!*" shouted Buldy Jones.

"Oh, mee Gord!" gasped Horse Wilson, collapsing weakly upon a bench.

II

In honor of the great event Buldy Jones gave a little dinner in his studio; and here I had the chance to get a good look at Juliana and become acquainted with her. She was not very pretty, but one forgot that after the first five minutes; indeed, would not have had her different for the prettiest face in all Paris. It goes without saying that she was smartly dressed, but neither did that count for much. Juliana was a squirrel in its wheel, a bird in its cage, a butterfly in its sunshine; she was perpetual motion—eyes, tongue, hand, wits were in one unending quiver. She effervesced, she bubbled; nimbleness that puzzled sight and sense was hers, and agility that stupefied, and delicate, swift little flashes that dazzled you and entranced you. So that in ten minutes' time I was in love with her, and I, too, became one of the band, content—no, delighted—to "fetch-and-carry" for her.

But that evening was not one of unalloyed gaiety. A complication had arisen. As everyone knows, there are two page's parts in *Van Arteveldt*, both equally important. Juliana was cast for one of these, but Bismarck that evening brought the news that another debutante, a niece of one of the directors of the Opera House, was to sing the other. This debutante's name was Straus, mademoiselle or madame we did not know, nor whether it was Anne, or Mariette, or Angélique-Henriette-de-Rohan-de-Pompadour; just Straus, flat, crude, stubborn, Teuton Straus. There she was, Straus, a great block of stone come smash into all our hopes and delicately woven plans and intrigues.

"Name-of-a-name!" exclaimed Bayard (the Frenchman), when Bismarck had delivered himself of this news.

"'Ere's a rum go, for fair," cried Horse Wilson.

"Dose ting!" exclaimed Bismarck. "Say, dose ting, dey meks me soh sick bei der stomach in. Der Herr Direktor will hev der *claque* enstructud, *nicht wahr?* Ach sure. Und der Straus will to der roof be upplaudut, and vat we get? Vat Juliana get? Nodding, bei Gott!"

"What do you think, Buldy?" said I.

"We're stuck," he observed.

"Oh, *mon p'tit* Buldy!" exclaimed Juliana, and with that began to cry.

"Is it as bad as all that?" I asked of Bayard in French.

"Ah, I believe you," he answered in the same language. "No chance. The director will do his possible to achieve an unbelievable success for this kind of a bad canary. It is as he says, this Bismarck. The director will instruct Roubauld—that's the *chef de claque*—to *bissé* Straus and to acclaim Juliana—not at all. This Roubauld gives the note to the *claque,* the *claque* gives the note to the audience, the audience gives the note to Paris, and Paris gives the note to the world, *et puis voilà.* No chance."

"So Roubauld rather commands the situation?"

"Roubauld," observed Bismarck, "iss der kaiser von der Frainch Ubera. He hes der bower oaf a Bersian satrap mit der resbonsipilitee oaf a veaning beby."

"Oh, he's a czar, right enough," commented Buldy Jones. "He never even appears in the Opera House. Works through his lieutenants. No one knows who *they* are. Places them in a part of the house where the *claque* can see 'em, and manages the business with a code of signals."

"As how?"

"Well, let's say he wants only a moderate applause. He pulls his moustache, or something like that, and next day the *Figaro* says: 'The audience at the debut of Mme. So-and-So, *"se trouva un peu froid"* (found itself a trifle chilly).' Vigorous applause, he adjusts his opera glasses. Enthusiasm, he uses his handkerchief. There you are. Francisque Sarcey! what does he count for—or the singer's voice? Not a bit of it. Reputations are made by the twirling of a moustache, and the world recognizes a God-given voice by a man blowing his nose."

"Why not buy Roubauld?"

"Son, I'm not rich enough."

"Well, pack the *claque.* The students——"

"We hef tink oaf dose ting long dime," said Bismarck. "Vhere dose *claqueurs* sit? Bei der *fauteuils d'orchestre,* eh? Well, *dere* you must vear der evenun dress oder you shall not be admit. How menny dose stoodunts you tink der evenun dress gehabt?"

The objection was unanswerable.

III

All this was only a fortnight before Juliana's debut. The week passed, and then ten days, and at last we had come to two days before the great night. We had been able to do nothing. Horse Wilson had observed that "'ere was a proper mess," and one and all we agreed with him. Juliana had made up her mind to go through with it as best she might, and trust to luck and her own talents. Already the other debutante was being boomed, and when the posters came out her name was in huge letters, large even as that of Escalais, who sang the leading role, while Juliana's did not even appear at all.

On the second day before the performance Buldy Jones and I walked to St. Cloud and took a very late luncheon at a little cafe in the town. The kismet that watched over Juliana plainly directed our steps thither, for before we had left the place we had made a most important discovery. It was luck—sheer, inconceivable, unprecedented bull luck—of the kind that takes your breath away, and as often as not so dumfounds you that you are unable to act on it. But—kismet again—it was part of this wonderful luck that we had the sense to use it. We had finished our luncheon and were burning the sugar for our coffee when Buldy Jones fell into conversation with the man who played the violin in a little four-piece orchestra that had been strumming and scraping in the back of the cafe for half an hour previous. I do not remember now what started their talk, nor do I remember how the subject of the *claque* of the Grand Opera House was introduced, but all at once—a bolt from the blue—I heard:

"Ah, yes, it is I who am the *sous-chef* for the week. In the day-time I perform upon the violin at this cafe, but in the evenings, hah, *autre chose*, I direct the *claque* at the Opera."

"Well, well! You don't tell me," said Buldy Jones. "Quite so; the *cuk-cuk claque.* I would very well wish, monsieur, to offer you something to drink."

We drank with the *sous-chef* of the *claque* of the Opera, and the drink was *Veuve Cliquot.* We were stupefied with admiration at the manner of his playing of the violin. We allowed him to pretend that he was quite a figure in the *beau monde,* and, ah, we assured him that in the next Franco-German War the cuirassiers would stable their horses in the Reichstag buildings of Berlin. He lived in the Rue du Temple, *numero* 20, did this indiscreet *sous-chef*; that also we found out (in case of emergency), and he would be at his post in the cafe of St. Cloud until five o'clock of the evening on which Juliana was to make her bow to the audience of the Opera. Would he not permit us to invite him to dine with us that evening? Indeed, he would be charmed. At this very cafe? As the gentlemen wished. Till Monday, then. Till Monday, *bien entendue*; and we parted from him and retired around the corner and leaned against the wall to get our bearings, and to be assured that we yet trod the stable earth.

"He's Roubauld's man," faltered Buldy Jones.

"The minion of the potentate."

"We—we—we—*got* him. We got the man who's got the *claque.*"

"But, Buldy, do we *dare?*"

"Oh, Lord!" exclaimed Buldy, "I don't know. Oh, man, if we—we *could* suppress him—at the last moment—on Juliana's night, the *claque* won't know what to do, and Juliana will break even with Straus, and that's all we want."

IV

We found the "band" at Julien's pottering over their *esquisses* for the week, and our talk was long and vehement. We felt like a committee of insurrectionists plotting countermoves.

As a result of it all, Bismarck, Horse Wilson, Bayard, Buldy Jones, and I foregathered in the cafe at St. Cloud about four hours before the curtain went up on the first act of *Van Arteveldt.* The *sous-chef* was there, and Buldy Jones began ordering a dinner that consisted chiefly of things to drink. Halfway through, Bismarck raised his champagne glass.

"*Gesundheit!*" he exclaimed. "*Gesundheit,* Devanbez." (This was the *sous-chef's* name.) "Hier iss der goot success oaf der yunge leddy vat meks der debut tonight, eh?"

"Ah, the mademoiselle who sings the role of the page."

"Yes," observed Buldy Jones; "we hope you will give her all the encouragement she deserves, Monsieur Devanbez."

"You may count on me, messieurs."

"Which," muttered Horse Wilson in English, "is just what we won't do, you bally old rotter."

"Fill 'em up again," said Buldy Jones, when the toast had been drunk. "I've a better one to propose."

We filled them up and proposed "The *Claque*"; we filled them a third time, and proposed "The Opera"; we filled them a fourth time, and—standing—gave "*L'Armée Française.*" It was then that Devanbez began to sing the "Marseillaise," and we shook hands furtively under the table, for we saw the beginning of the end.

When he developed oblique and scathing sarcasm in his remarks to Bismarck, interspersed with terrible observations as to Alsace and *la revanche,* we concluded that our cause was won. It was about quarter to seven.

"Aha!" Devanbez was saying. "Wait then a little, you others, you Prussians. The lion sleeps, the lion of Belfort. When he shall awake himself"—he struck a terrific attitude—"he will in one mouthful eat you, thus." He devoured an olive—pit and all—at a gulp.

"He freezes me with terror, this man," murmured Bayard.

But Bismarck was particularly touchy on his nationality, and at this promptly remembered that he was a German.

"Pouf! paf! Dot line von Bailvoort!" he said to us derisively. "Unzer Fritz hev alretty yet long dime cut der claws of him. If dose Frainch soldier coom cross der frontier, say, I tell you vat ve do, ve Broosians, ve hev der boliceman arrest 'em."

Devanbez, understanding only that he was set at naught, leaped up.

"What-is-that-which-it-is-what?" he vociferated. "I tell you the next time Bazaine will not betray us. Ah, no, Germany is going to have the bad quarter of an hour——"

Buldy Jones had to interfere to prevent hostilities.

We left the cafe, taking Devanbez between Buldy Jones and myself, and walked through the woods in the direction of the railway station. By that time Devanbez was no longer a factor to be considered in the affair of Juliana's debut. His hat fell off twice. Each time Buldy Jones picked it up and clapped it upon his head.

At the station we learned that the Southern Express from Paris to Châlons was due in about five minutes. Buldy Jones bought a ticket to Châlons and return, and put twenty-five francs into the vest pocket of Devanbez, *sous-chef de claque*. We had no more than time to complete these arrangements when the train charged into the station.

"Up with you," said Buldy to Devanbez. "The Paris train, monsieur. Here's your ticket. *Bon voyage!* Steady! Not there—you bought *first* class, don't you remember? In with you! Guard! Where's the guard? Here, this man, our friend, is to get down at Châlons, understand? You're off, Devanbez. Good-bye."

"*Au plaisir de vous revoir, messieurs! Hoopla! à bas Bismarck! Vive la République!*

> "*Allons, enfants de la patrie,*
> *Le jour de gloire———*"

But as the train drew away Bismarck shouted after it: "*Hoch der Vaterland! Hoch der Kaiser!* Doand you forged to *bissé* Straus tonight."

V

Shall I ever forget that night—the night of Juliana's debut! Looking back at it now it resolves itself into one stupendous blur of unfamiliar sights, into one vast blare of confused and raucous noises. I know now just how the First Consul felt when he faced the throng in the Hall of the Ancients, frightened at the uproar he had unchained, at the pandemonium he had provoked, but with just enough courage to face the music, just enough daring to carry out the plan that might succeed, or that might collapse.

After we had sent Devanbez off to Châlons, we thought for the moment (as the train carried us back to Paris) that we had brought off our coup, that we had done the best we could. But all at once Buldy Jones complicated the situation still further.

"Look here," he said abruptly; "I'm not saying much, but what do you think of that?"

With the words he exhibited two or three slips of paper, with the air of one who flourishes a banner. We looked at them stupidly.

"I s'y, ol' chap," said the Horse, "what's it all abaout? Get on with it. What's these?"

"This," said Buldy Jones, holding up a blue oblong of pasteboard, "is the ticket for Devanbez's seat. *Will* you look where he sits?"

"*Sapristi!*" murmured Bayard, as he looked at it. "He has a box, the ruffian."

"No," said Buldy Jones, "*we* have it. Now, then, cast your eye on this. I found this and the tickets in his hat. 'Member, it kept falling off?"

"*Du Lieber Gott!*" exclaimed Bismarck.

"Why, man alive!" cried Horse Wilson. "Why, Buldy Jones! S'y, strike me straight. *It's the code.*"

"Right you are, m'son. It's the signals he uses to direct the *claque*, and *we got 'em.*"

"But, oh, s'y, what a rummy go! Buldy, y' can't, y' don't mean to s'y that—that—oh, my aunt!—that you're going to *use* 'em?"

"Son," said Buldy Jones, tapping his chest, "watch me."

We boomed into Paris on the stroke of seven-thirty, we hacked it across the city *ventre-à-terre* to the Maison Lafitte, caught the proprietor in the act of shutting up, and rented and donned four abominable dress suits, four broken opera hats, and four pairs of gruesome white gloves. Breathless, hysterical, shambling in our rented plumage, we debouched into a box in the second tier next the stage, were kicked into a realization of our surroundings by Buldy Jones, and sat up with quaking hearts to face the glitter, the murmur, and the perfume of *le tout* Paris. The overture was being played.

"Buck up, buck up!" adjured Horse Wilson. "No need of funking."

"That's what I say," growled Buldy Jones. "We're losing our nerve when we hold a straight ace-high. Now, attention. I'm going to try 'em."

The overture was drawing to a close. We could see the *claque* perfectly well, two rows of the *fauteuils d'orchestre* filled with solemn nondescripts in dress suits (that, like ours, were, no doubt, rented or borrowed), melancholy harlequins, stuffers, bought like dishonest voters in an election at home.

"Steady now," muttered Buldy Jones. "I guess we think that overture rather nifty. What's the signal?—oh, I remember."

The eyes of the harlequins were furtively turned to our box. The overture closed with a flourish of violins and a ruffle of the snare drum, and Buldy Jones passed his hand through his hair. Instantly a loud, well-sustained clapping of hands developed. The *claque* was obedient, and a little after the audience followed its lead. The leader of the orchestra turned about and bowed. The *claque* still applauded.

"Here, down brakes," said Buldy Jones. "He don't need to get it all."

"Right, oh," muttered Horse Wilson. "Shut 'em off. Shut 'em off. They'll keep it up all night if you don't."

Buldy Jones folded his arms. Promptly the applause died away, and the leader of the orchestra, left stranded in the middle of a bow, returned precipitately to his seat and tapped for the prelude.

The curtain rose and the opera began. A chorus by the burgesses of Ghent was followed by an aria and *recitatif* by the captain of the city watch. Then the sister of Van Arteveldt and her confidante appeared and sang a trio with the captain; after this the sister was left alone (the part was that of the Leading Lady, and was sung by Escalais herself)—and intoned an elaborate solo.

"S'y, give her a show," said Horse Wilson, "she's doing her best."

"All right," answered Buldy, who was familiar with the opera. "She has a high note along in here pretty soon. I'll touch 'em up then. Ah, there it is!" He stroked his hair, absolute silence; he repeated the motion, no response; and poor Escalais, who seldom failed to get a hand at this point, was forced to go on with but a feeble flutter from isolated corners of the house, for the audience, depending on the *claque,* unquestionably followed its lead.

"Say, then," exclaimed Bayard, "there is something which does not go."

"Some blyme thing wrong," observed Horse Wilson. "Where's your bloomin' code?"

Buldy Jones put his hand to his pocket, then turned suddenly pale.

"Boys," he gasped, "I left it in my other pocket when I changed at Lafittte's. I was working these first signals from memory."

VI

"*Himmel!*" groaned Bismarck.

"And Straus and Juliana both come on in the very next scene," I cried. "There, the chorus is coming back, and here comes the Duchess of Ghent; the Queen and court come on in a jiffy."

All at once the *claque* roared to the roof; there were even cries of *bis, bis*. The acclamation came squarely in the middle of a chorus of old men, a number that was only a "filler" and never applauded.

"What did you do? What did you do, Buldy?" cried Horse Wilson.

"I don't know. Here's the devil to pay. *I'm making signals without knowing it.* Darn fool *claqueurs*, they'd yell *encore* in the *entr'acte* if they got the tip. I—oh, Lord! there they go again."

"Shut 'em oop. Shut 'em oop den."

"Dammit, I've folded me arms till I'm black in the face. They must have two codes, an' we only got the wrong one, somehow, or only got part of it right. *I* don't know, I'm all mixed up."

Suddenly the *claque* stopped with terrifying abruptness, and the music on the stage made itself heard again. We could see the leader of the orchestra looking distressfully at the *claque*, and on Escalais's face there was a sign of gathering wrath. Twice within the next three minutes Buldy started applause at the most inopportune moments. It was precisely as though a party of children were playing with the levers and throttles of a locomotive. The house began to grow uneasy. There were cries of "*Assez! Assez!*" from the gallery.

Then all at once Juliana appeared. She wore the costume of a page, and was supposed to deliver a note from the queen to the captain. The presentation gave her the excuse for her entrance song.

She began to sing, and that, too, surprisingly well. She was not nervous. The audience fell quiet.

"Now den," whispered Bismarck to Buldy Jones, "tink oaf sometings. Der *claque* hev der eye on you."

Now there is a pause in the first page's song, between the first and second movements, while the orchestra elaborates the motif, and it is just here that the singer should get her first hand. Also at the same point the second page—which was Straus—is supposed to enter at the back. Later on she takes stage and interrupts the first page, has a song of her own, and the number closes with a trio between the two pages and the captain of the watch. After this enter the queen and all the court. It is the finale of the first act.

But as Juliana was singing the last bars of the first part of her song Buldy Jones saw that the *claque* was not going to applaud. Again and again he stroked his hair, fluttered his handkerchief, pulled his moustache, nodded, winked, coughed—all to no purpose. The *claque* remained impassive. They were waiting for their signal. They would obey us implicitly. In a second it would be too late. This was Juliana's principal number. We held the key of the position, and we were powerless.

"Lord, I can't start 'em!" groaned Buldy Jones.

"Maybe," I hazarded, "the audience will applaud of itself."

"*Niemals*," groaned Bismarck. "We hev in der tsoup gefallen."

Just as Juliana was on the last notes there were hurried steps in the corridor outside, the door of the box was flung open, and there stood, not the *sous-chef*, not Devanbez, but the satrap, the autocrat, the czar himself, Roubauld.

"Oh, the bounder!" exclaimed Horse Wilson.

Buldy Jones turned about, saw Roubauld, rose to his feet, and in the movement the *claque* saw its signal and burst out into such a tempest of applause that the chandelier shook again.

But Roubauld was a general. He took in the situation at a glance, and before he deigned to notice us stepped to the front of the box and made some barely perceptible gesture. The *claque* knew its master, and cowered to silence.

We saw our victory turned into defeat, but in the next second, and before Roubauld could speak, Horse Wilson cried:

"*Hi, we've started the house for fair, and you can't work that, old man!*"

It was true; the *claque had* started the audience before Roubauld could interfere, and a very creditable applause was under way from gallery, loge, and orchestra.

Then Roubauld did a daring thing. His authority was at stake, the wrong debutante was being encored; his machine was cracking; he was desperate. His signal was so cleverly given that none of us perceived it; but the *claque* that the minute before had been tumultuous in applause, recognized it, and began to hiss and call, "*Assez! Assez!*" Part of the audience followed suit; but we in our box suddenly burst out into shouts of—

"*Bis, bis! Encore, très bien, brava Juliana!*"

And just at this, of all moments, Straus made her entrance.

VII

The *claque*, obedient to Roubauld's direction, began a vociferous demonstration, but by now the people in *our* part of the audience, Juliana's part, seemed, as Horse Wilson put it afterward, to "pipe the whole gyme." They answered the *claque* shout for shout, cheering where they hissed, crying "*Encore!*" to their "*Assez!*"

Part of the house was shouting "Juliana," part "Straus," while another part, feeling itself exploited, began to vociferate:

"*À bas la claque! À bas la claque!*"

The whole opera was interrupted. Helpless, the leader of the orchestra sat in his place, his baton swinging uselessly at his side. The singers on the stage stared blankly out into the tumult.

Through the open door at the back of our box entered four gendarmes. Roubauld, with the air of a Richelieu, indicated us.

"These are the people," he said. "*Mettez ces gens, à la porte.*"

"Gyme's up," said Horse Wilson with philosophy.

But when one of the officers put his hand on Bismarck's arm the Prussian suddenly trumpeted like an elephant.

"Gedt oudt, *Bube*. Gedt oudt, *Spitzbuch*. Tek der hend away off me." Then, suddenly losing his wits altogether, thundered: "Me, I am den Broosian! I doand be arrest bei no demn Frainchman! *À bas la France. Hoch der Kaiser!*"

In a twinkling a dozen voices from the gallery yelled:

"*À bas l'Allemagne! Vive la France!*"

"*À la porte, à la porte le Prussien!*"

"*À la porte, la sale tête!*"

Our box was in full view of the audience, and everyone could see Bismarck and the gendarmes grappling with each other. Below us, in a box of the first tier, a lady screamed. In the amphitheater whole parties, scandalized at the uproar, were getting out. A nervous little gentleman in evening dress, who evidently mistook the whole situation and believed a panic impended, appeared on the stage, exclaiming from time to time:

"*Messieurs, mesdames, un peu de silence. Il n'y a pas de danger; messieurs, je vous prie, il n'y a pas de feu.* There is no fire, sit down."

Fire. It was the fatal word. No doubt three fourths of the audience knew the small gentleman was confused. Not so the remaining fourth. There was no panic, but some three or four hundred people left the building. They did not stand on the order of their going, and the more they were reasoned with the angrier they became.

In a single glance over the auditorium I saw four fistfights going on in different quarters of the building. Fully a hundred men in the gallery were standing on their feet shouting:

"*Vive la France! À bas l'Allemagne!*"

Others vociferated:

"*À la porte, à la porte!*"

The *claque*—Roman soldiers in the destruction of Pompeii— still kept up an incessant: "Straus! Straus!" while from gallery and pit came answering calls of:

"*Encore! Bis, bis! Très bien!*"

"*Hoch der Kaiser!*" bellowed Bismarck.

"No fire. No fire. Sit down, *messieurs,*" pleaded the little man from the stage.

And in the midst of this clamor, this swirl of confusion, the curtain fell.

We were duly and formally arrested, and passed the night in the prison of Saint Lazare. The next morning Buldy Jones paid our fines, and by noon we were once more our own men. But we were no sooner liberated than Buldy Jones marched us to the nearest kiosk and bought the morning's *Figaro*. The article we sought for read as follows:

"At the performance of *Van Arteveldt*, at the Opera last night, a young debutante, whose stage name appears to be Mlle. Juliana, acquitted herself of her role with astonishing credit. Her first song was received with acclamation, and, indeed, it is almost permissible to add that the young lady created a veritable furor.

"A party of intoxicated German students took this occasion to insult the Republic, and were arrested by the gendarmes. Unfortunately the audience misunderstood the cause of the disturbance, and believing that a conflagration was at hand, left the building. There was no panic. The German students were arrested. It is not believed that the affair will engender any grave international complications."

A DEAL IN WHEAT

I

THE BEAR—WHEAT AT SIXTY-TWO

As Sam Lewiston backed the horse into the shafts of his buckboard and began hitching the tugs to the whiffletree, his wife came out from the kitchen door of the house and drew near, and stood for some time at the horse's head, her arms folded and her apron rolled around them. For a long moment neither spoke. They had talked over the situation so long and so comprehensively the night before that there seemed to be nothing more to say.

The time was late in the summer, the place a ranch in southwestern Kansas, and Lewiston and his wife were two of a vast population of farmers, wheat growers, who at that moment were passing through a crisis—a crisis that at any moment might culminate in tragedy. Wheat was down to sixty-six.

At length Emma Lewiston spoke.

"Well," she hazarded, looking vaguely out across the ranch toward the horizon, leagues distant; "well, Sam, there's always that offer of brother Joe's. We can quit—and go to Chicago—if the worst comes."

"And give up!" exclaimed Lewiston, running the lines through the torets. "Leave the ranch! Give up! After all these years!"

His wife made no reply for the moment. Lewiston climbed into the buckboard and gathered up the lines. "Well, here goes for the last try, Emmie," he said. "Good-bye, girl. Maybe things will look better in town today."

"Maybe," she said gravely. She kissed her husband good-bye and stood for some time looking after the buckboard traveling toward the town in a moving pillar of dust.

"I don't know," she murmured at length; "I don't know just how we're going to make out."

When he reached town, Lewiston tied the horse to the iron railing in front of the Odd Fellows' Hall, the ground floor of which was occupied by the post office, and went across the street and up the stairway of a building of brick and granite—quite the most pretentious structure of the town—and knocked at a door upon the first landing. The door was furnished with a pane of frosted glass, on which, in gold letters, was inscribed, "Bridges & Co., Grain Dealers."

Bridges himself, a middle-aged man who wore a velvet skull-cap and who was smoking a Pittsburgh stogie, met the farmer at the counter and the two exchanged perfunctory greetings.

"Well," said Lewiston tentatively, after a while.

"Well, Lewiston," said the other, "I can't take that wheat of yours at any better than sixty-two."

"Sixty-*two!*"

"It's the Chicago price that does it, Lewiston. Truslow is bearing the stuff for all he's worth. It's Truslow and the bear clique that stick the knife into us. The price broke again this morning. We've just got a wire."

"Good heavens," murmured Lewiston, looking vaguely from side to side. "That—that ruins me. I *can't* carry my grain any longer—what with storage charges and—and—— Bridges, I don't see just how I'm going to make out. Sixty-two cents a bushel! Why, man, what with this and with that it's cost me nearly a dollar a bushel to raise that wheat, and now Truslow——"

He turned away abruptly with a quick gesture of infinite discouragement.

He went down the stairs, and making his way to where his buckboard was hitched, got in, and, with eyes vacant, the reins slipping and sliding in his limp, half-open hands, drove slowly back to the ranch. His wife had seen him coming, and met him as he drew up before the barn.

"Well?" she demanded.

"Emmie," he said as he got out of the buckboard, laying his arm across her shoulder, "Emmie, I guess we'll take up with Joe's offer. We'll go to Chicago. We're cleaned out!"

II
THE BULL—WHEAT AT A DOLLAR-TEN

...——*and said Party of the Second Part further covenants and agrees to merchandise such wheat in foreign ports, it being understood and agreed between the Party of the First Part and the Party of the Second Part that the wheat hereinbefore mentioned is released and sold to the Party of the Second Part for export purposes only, and not for consumption or distribution within the boundaries of the United States of America or of Canada.*

"Now, Mr. Gates, if you will sign for Mr. Truslow I guess that'll be all," remarked Hornung when he had finished reading.

Hornung affixed his signature to the two documents and passed them over to Gates, who signed for his principal and client, Truslow—or, as he had been called ever since he had gone into the fight against Hornung's corner—the Great Bear. Hornung's secretary was called in and witnessed the signatures, and Gates thrust the contract into his Gladstone bag and stood up, smoothing his hat.

"You will deliver the warehouse receipts for the grain," began Gates.

"I'll send a messenger to Truslow's office before noon," interrupted Hornung. "You can pay by certified check through the Illinois Trust people."

When the other had taken himself off, Hornung sat for some moments gazing abstractedly toward his office windows, thinking over the whole matter. He had just agreed to release to Truslow, at the rate of one dollar and ten cents per bushel, one hundred thousand out of the two million and odd bushels of wheat that he, Hornung, controlled, or actually owned. And for the moment he was wondering if, after all, he had done wisely in not goring the Great Bear to actual financial death. He had made him pay one hundred thousand dollars. Truslow was good for this amount. Would it not have been better to have put a prohibitive figure on the grain and forced the Bear into bankruptcy? True, Hornung would then be without his enemy's money, but Truslow would have been eliminated from the situation, and that—so Hornung told himself—was always a consummation most devoutly, strenuously and diligently to be striven for. Truslow once dead was dead, but the Bear was never more dangerous than when desperate.

"But so long as he can't get *wheat*," muttered Hornung at the end of his reflections, "he can't hurt me. And he can't get it. That I *know*."

For Hornung controlled the situation. So far back as the February of that year an "unknown bull" had been making his presence felt on the floor of the Board of Trade. By the middle of March the commercial reports of the daily press had begun to speak of "the powerful bull clique"; a few weeks later that legendary condition of affairs implied and epitomized in the magic words "Dollar Wheat" had been attained, and by the first of April, when the price had been boosted to one dollar and ten cents a bushel, Hornung had disclosed his hand, and in place of mere rumors, the definite and authoritative news that May wheat had been cornered in the Chicago pit went flashing around the world from Liverpool to Odessa and from Duluth to Buenos Aires.

It was—so the veteran operators were persuaded—Truslow himself who had made Hornung's corner possible. The Great Bear had for once overreached himself, and, believing himself all-powerful, had hammered the price just the fatal fraction too far down. Wheat had gone to sixty-two—for the time, and under the circumstances, an abnormal price. When the reaction came it was tremendous. Hornung saw his chance, seized it, and in a few months had turned the tables, had cornered the product, and virtually driven the bear clique out of the pit.

On the same day that the delivery of the hundred thousand bushels was made to Truslow, Hornung met his broker at his lunch club.

"Well," said the latter, "I see you let go that line of stuff to Truslow."

Hornung nodded; but the broker added:

"Remember, I was against it from the very beginning. I know we've cleared up over a hundred thou'. I would have fifty times preferred to have lost twice that and *smashed Truslow dead*. Bet you what you like he makes us pay for it somehow."

"Huh!" grunted his principal. "How about insurance, and

warehouse charges, and carrying expenses on that lot? Guess we'd have had to pay those, too, if we'd held on."

But the other put up his chin, unwilling to be persuaded. "I won't sleep easy," he declared, "till Truslow is busted."

III
THE PIT

Just as Going mounted the steps on the edge of the pit the great gong struck, a roar of a hundred voices developed with the swiftness of successive explosions, the rush of a hundred men surging downward to the center of the pit filled the air with the stamp and grind of feet, a hundred hands in eager strenuous gestures tossed upward from out the brown of the crowd, the official reporter in his cage on the margin of the pit leaned far forward with straining ear to catch the opening bid, and another day of battle was begun.

Since the sale of the hundred thousand bushels of wheat to Truslow the "Hornung crowd" had steadily shouldered the price higher until on this particular morning it stood at one dollar and a half. That was Hornung's price. No one else had any grain to sell.

But not ten minutes after the opening, Going was surprised out of all countenance to hear shouted from the other side of the pit these words:

"Sell May at one-fifty."

Going was for the moment touching elbows with Kimbark on one side and with Merriam on the other, all three belonging to the "Hornung crowd." Their answering challenge of "*Sold*" was as the voice of one man. They did not pause to reflect upon the strangeness of the circumstance. (That was for afterward.) Their response to the offer was as unconscious as reflex action and almost as rapid, and before the pit was well aware of what had happened the transaction of one thousand bushels was down upon Going's trading card and fifteen hundred dollars had changed hands. But here was a marvel—the whole available supply of wheat cornered, Hornung master of the situation, invincible, unassailable;

yet behold a man willing to sell, a bear bold enough to raise his head.

"That was Kennedy, wasn't it, who made that offer?" asked Kimbark, as Going noted down the trade—"Kennedy, that new man?"

"Yes; who do you suppose he's selling for? Who's willing to go short at this stage of the game?"

"Maybe he ain't short."

"Short! Great heavens, man; where'd he get the stuff?"

"Blamed if I know. We can account for every handful of May. Steady! Oh, there he goes again."

"Sell a thousand May at one-fifty," vociferated the bear broker, throwing out his hand, one finger raised to indicate the number of "contracts" offered. This time it was evident that he was attacking the Hornung crowd deliberately, for, ignoring the jam of traders that swept toward him, he looked across the pit to where Going and Kimbark were shouting "*Sold! Sold!*" and nodded his head.

A second time Going made memoranda of the trade, and either the Hornung holdings were increased by two thousand bushels of May wheat or the Hornung bank account swelled by at least three thousand dollars of some unknown short's money.

Of late—so sure was the bull crowd of its position—no one had even thought of glancing at the inspection sheet on the bulletin board. But now one of Going's messengers hurried up to him with the announcement that this sheet showed receipts at Chicago for that morning of twenty-five thousand bushels, and not credited to Hornung. Someone had got hold of a line of wheat overlooked by the "clique" and was dumping it upon them.

"Wire the Chief," said Going over his shoulder to Merriam. This one struggled out of the crowd, and on a telegraph blank scribbled:

> "Strong bear movement—New man—Kennedy—
> selling in lots of five contracts—Chicago receipts
> twenty-five thousand."

The message was dispatched, and in a few moments the answer came back, laconic, of military terseness:

> "Support the market."

And Going obeyed, Merriam and Kimbark following, the new broker fairly throwing the wheat at them in thousand-bushel lots.

"Sell May at 'fifty; sell May; sell May." A moment's indecision, an instant's hesitation, the first faint suggestion of weakness, and the market would have broken under them. But for the better part of four hours they stood their ground, taking all that was offered, in constant communication with the Chief, and from time to time stimulated and steadied by his brief, unvarying command:

"Support the market."

At the close of the session they had bought in the twenty-five thousand bushels of May. Hornung's position was as stable as a rock, and the price closed even with the opening figure—one dollar and a half.

But the morning's work was the talk of all La Salle Street. Who was back of the raid? What was the meaning of this unexpected selling? For weeks the pit trading had been merely nominal. Truslow, the Great Bear, from whom the most serious attack might have been expected, had gone to his country seat at Geneva Lake, in Wisconsin, declaring himself to be out of the market entirely. He went bass-fishing every day.

IV

THE BELT LINE

On a certain day toward the middle of the month, at a time when the mysterious Bear had unloaded some eighty thousand bushels upon Hornung, a conference was held in the library of Hornung's home. His broker attended it, and also a clean-faced, bright-eyed individual whose name of Cyrus Ryder might have been found upon the payroll of a rather well-known detective agency. For upward of half an hour after the conference began the detective spoke, the other two listening attentively, gravely.

"Then, last of all," concluded Ryder, "I made out I was a hobo, and began stealing rides on the Belt Line Railroad. Know the road? It just circles Chicago. Truslow owns it. Yes? Well, then I began to catch on. I noticed that cars of certain numbers—thirty-one nought thirty-four, thirty-two one ninety—well, the numbers don't matter, but anyhow, these cars were always switched onto the sidings by Mr. Truslow's main elevator D soon as they came in. The wheat was shunted in, and they were pulled out again. Well, I spotted one car and stole a ride on her. Say, look here, *that car went right around the city on the Belt, and came back to D again, and the same wheat in her all the time.* The grain was re-inspected—it was raw, I tell you—and the warehouse receipts made out just as though the stuff had come in from Kansas or Iowa."

"The same wheat all the time!" interrupted Hornung.

"The same wheat—your wheat, that you sold to Truslow."

"Great snakes!" ejaculated Hornung's broker. "Truslow never took it abroad at all."

"Took it abroad! Say, he's just been running it around Chicago, like the supers in 'shenandoah,' round an' round, so you'd think it was a new lot, an' selling it back to you again."

"No wonder we couldn't account for so much wheat."

"Bought it from us at one-ten, and made us buy it back—our own wheat—at one-fifty."

Hornung and his broker looked at each other in silence for a moment. Then all at once Hornung struck the arm of his chair with his fist and exploded in a roar of laughter. The broker stared for one bewildered moment, then followed his example.

"Sold! Sold!" shouted Hornung almost gleefully. "Upon my soul it's as good as a Gilbert and Sullivan show. And we——— Oh, Lord! Billy, shake on it, and hats off to my distinguished friend, Truslow. He'll be President someday. Hey! What? Prosecute him? Not I."

"He's done us out of a neat hatful of dollars for all that," observed the broker, suddenly grave.

"Billy, it's worth the price."

"We've got to make it up somehow."

"Well, tell you what. We were going to boost the price to one seventy-five next week, and make that our settlement figure."

"Can't do it now. Can't afford it."

"No. Here; we'll let out a big link; we'll put wheat at two dollars, and let it go at that."

"Two it is, then," said the broker.

V

THE BREAD LINE

The street was very dark and absolutely deserted. It was a district on the "South Side," not far from the Chicago River, given up largely to wholesale stores, and after nightfall was empty of all life. The echoes slept but lightly hereabouts, and the slightest footfall, the faintest noise, woke them upon the instant and sent them clamoring up and down the length of the pavement between the iron-shuttered fronts. The only light visible came from the side door of a certain "Vienna" bakery, where at one o'clock in the morning loaves of bread were given away to any who should ask. Every evening about nine o'clock the outcasts began to gather about the side door. The stragglers came in rapidly, and the line— the "bread line," as it was called—began to form. By midnight it was usually some hundred yards in length, stretching almost the entire length of the block.

Toward ten in the evening, his coat collar turned up against the fine drizzle that pervaded the air, his hands in his pockets, his elbows gripping his sides, Sam Lewiston came up and silently took his place at the end of the line.

Unable to conduct his farm upon a paying basis at the time when Truslow, the "Great Bear," had sent the price of grain down to sixty-two cents a bushel, Lewiston had turned over his entire property to his creditors, and, leaving Kansas for good, had abandoned farming, and had left his wife at her sister's boardinghouse in Topeka with the understanding that she was to join him in Chicago so soon as he had found a steady job. Then he had come to Chicago and had turned workman. His brother Joe conducted a small hat factory on Archer Avenue, and for a time he found there a meager employment. But difficulties had occurred, times were bad, the hat factory was involved in debts, the repealing of a certain import duty on manufactured felt overcrowded the home market with cheap Belgian and French products, and in the end his brother had assigned and gone to Milwaukee.

Thrown out of work, Lewiston drifted aimlessly about Chicago, from pillar to post, working a little, earning here a dollar, there a dime, but always sinking, sinking, till at last the ooze of the lowest bottom dragged at his feet and the rush of the great ebb went over him and engulfed him and shut him out from the light, and a park bench became his home and the "bread line" his chief makeshift of subsistence.

He stood now in the enfolding drizzle, sodden, stupefied with fatigue. Before and behind stretched the line. There was no talking. There was no sound. The street was empty. It was so still that the passing of a cable car in the adjoining thoroughfare grated like prolonged rolling explosions, beginning and ending at immeasurable distances. The drizzle descended incessantly. After a long time midnight struck.

There was something ominous and gravely impressive in this interminable line of dark figures, close pressed, soundless; a crowd, yet absolutely still; a close-packed, silent file, waiting, waiting in the vast deserted night-ridden street; waiting without a word, without a movement, there under the night and under the slow-moving mists of rain.

Few in the crowd were professional beggars. Most of them were workmen, long since out of work, forced into idleness by long-continued "hard times," by ill luck, by sickness. To them the "bread line" was a godsend. At least they could not starve. Between jobs here in the end was something to hold them up—a small platform, as it were, above the sweep of black water, where for a moment they might pause and take breath before the plunge.

The period of waiting on this night of rain seemed endless to those silent, hungry men; but at length there was a stir. The line moved. The side door opened. Ah, at last! They were going to hand out the bread.

But instead of the usual white-aproned undercook with his crowded hampers there now appeared in the doorway a new man—a young fellow who looked like a bookkeeper's assistant. He bore in his hand a placard, which he tacked to the outside of the door. Then he disappeared within the bakery, locking the door after him.

A shudder of poignant despair, an unformed, inarticulate sense of calamity, seemed to run from end to end of the line. What had happened? Those in the rear, unable to read the placard, surged forward, a sense of bitter disappointment clutching at their hearts.

The line broke up, disintegrated into a shapeless throng—a throng that crowded forward and collected in front of the shut door whereon the placard was affixed. Lewiston, with the others, pushed forward. On the placard he read these words:

> "Owing to the fact that the price of grain has been increased to two dollars a bushel, there will be no distribution of bread from this bakery until further notice."

Lewiston turned away, dumb, bewildered. Till morning he walked the streets, going on without purpose, without direction. But now at last his luck had turned. Overnight the wheel of his fortunes had creaked and swung upon its axis, and before noon he had found a job in the street-cleaning brigade. In the course of time he rose to be first shift-boss, then deputy inspector, then inspector, promoted to the dignity of driving in a red wagon with rubber tires and drawing a salary instead of mere wages. The wife was sent for and a new start made.

But Lewiston never forgot. Dimly he began to see the significance of things. Caught once in the cogs and wheels of a great and terrible engine, he had seen—none better—its workings. Of all the men who had vainly stood in the "bread line" on that rainy night in early summer, he, perhaps, had been the only one who had struggled up to the surface again. How many others had gone down in the great ebb? Grim question; he dared not think how many.

He had seen the two ends of a great wheat operation—a battle between Bear and Bull. The stories (subsequently published in the city's press) of Truslow's countermove in selling Hornung his own wheat, supplied the unseen section. The farmer—he who raised the wheat—was ruined upon one hand; the working-man—he who consumed it—was ruined upon the other. But between the two, the great operators, who never saw the wheat they traded in, bought and sold the world's food, gambled in the nourishment of entire nations, practiced their tricks, their chi-

canery and oblique shifty "deals," were reconciled in their differ-
ences, and went on through their appointed way, jovial, contented,
enthroned, and unassailable.

THE DUAL PERSONALITY OF
SLICK DICK NICKERSON

I

On a certain morning in the spring of the year, the three men who were known as the Three Black Crows called at the office of "The President of the Pacific and Oriental Flotation Company," situated in an obscure street near San Francisco's waterfront. They were Strokher, the tall, blond, solemn, silent Englishman; Hardenberg, the American, dry of humor, shrewd, resourceful, who bargained like a Vermonter and sailed a schooner like a Gloucester cod-fisher; and in their company, as ever inseparable from the other two, came the little colonial, nicknamed, for occult reasons, "Ally Bazan," a small, wiry man, excitable, vociferous, who was without fear, without guile and without money.

When Hardenberg, who was always spokesman for the Three Crows, had sent in their names, they were admitted at once to the inner office of the "President." The President was an old man, bearded like a prophet, with watery blue eyes and a forehead wrinkled like an orang's. He spoke to the Three Crows in the manner of one speaking to friends he has not seen in some time.

"Well, Mr. Ryder," began Hardenberg. "We called around to see if you had anything fer us this morning. I don't mind telling you that we're at liberty jus' now. Anything doing?"

Ryder fingered his beard distressfully. "Very little, Joe; very little."

"Got any wrecks?"

"Not a wreck."

Hardenberg turned to a great map that hung on the wall by Ryder's desk. It was marked in places by red crosses, against which were written certain numbers and letters. Hardenberg put his finger on a small island south of the Marquesas group and demanded: "What might be H. 33, Mr. President?"

"Pearl Island," answered the President. "Davidson is on that job."

"Or H. 125?" Hardenberg indicated a point in the Gilbert group.

"Guano deposits. That's promised."

"Hallo! You're up in the Aleutians, I make out. 20 A.—what's that?"

"Old government telegraph wire—line abandoned—finest drawn-copper wire. I've had three boys at that for months."

"What's 301? This here, off the Mexican coast?"

The President, unable to remember, turned to his one clerk: "Hyers, what's 301? Isn't that Peterson?"

The clerk ran his finger down a column. "No, sir; 301 is the Whisky Ship."

"Ah! So it is. I remember. *You* remember, too, Joe. Little schooner, the *Tropic Bird*—sixty days out from Callao—five hundred cases of whisky aboard—sunk in squall. It was thirty years ago. Think of five hundred cases of thirty-year-old whisky! There's money in that if I can lay my hands on the schooner. Suppose you try that, you boys—on a twenty percent basis. Come now, what do you say?"

"Not for *five* percent," declared Hardenberg. "How'd we raise her? How'd we know how deep she lies? Not for Joe. What's the matter with landing arms down here in Central America for Bocas and his gang?"

"I'm out o' that, Joe. Too much competition."

"What's doing here in Tahiti—No. 88? It ain't lettered."

Once more the President consulted his books. "Ah!—88. Here we are. Cache o' illicit pearls. I had it looked up. Nothing in it."

"Say, Cap'n!"—Hardenberg's eye had traveled to the upper edge of the map—"whatever did you strike up here in Alaska? At Point Barrow, s'elp me Bob! It's 48 B."

The President stirred uneasily in his place. "Well, I ain't quite worked that scheme out, Joe. But I smell the deal. There's a Russian post along there some'eres. Where they catch sea otters. And the skins o' sea otters are selling this very day for seventy dollars at any port in China."

"I s'y," piped up Ally Bazan, "I knows a bit about that gyme. They's a bally kind o' Lum-tums among them Chinese as sports those syme skins on their bally clothes—as a mark o' rank, d'ye see?"

"Have you figured at all on the proposition, Cap'n?" inquired Hardenberg.

"There's risk in it, Joe; big risk," declared the President nervously. "But I'd only ask fifteen percent."

"You *have* worked out the scheme, then."

"Well—ah—y'see, there's the risk, and—ah——" Suddenly Ryder leaned forward, his watery blue eyes glinting: "Boys, it's a *jewel*. It's just your kind. I'd a-sent for you, to try on this very scheme, if you hadn't shown up. You kin have the *Bertha Millner*—I've a year's charter o' her from Wilbur—and I'll only ask you fifteen percent, of the *net* profits—*net*, mind you."

"I ain't buyin' no dead horse, Cap'n," returned Hardenberg, "but I'll say this: we pay no fifteen percent."

"Banks and the Ruggles were daft to try it and give me twenty-five."

"An' where would Banks land the scheme? I know him. You put him on that German cipher-code job down Honolulu way, an' it cost you about a thousand before you could pull out. We'll give you seven an' a half."

"Ten," declared Ryder, "ten, Joe, at the very least. Why, how much do you suppose just the stores would cost me? And Point Barrow—why, Joe, that's right up in the Arctic. I got to run the risk o' you getting the *Bertha* smashed in the ice."

"What do *we* risk?" retorted Hardenberg; and it was the monosyllabic Strokher who gave the answer:

"Chokee, by Jove!"

"Ten is fair. It's ten or nothing," answered Hardenberg.

"Gross, then, Joe. Ten on the gross—or I give the job to the Ruggles and Banks."

"Who's your bloomin' agent?" put in Ally Bazan.

"Nickerson. I sent him with Peterson on that *Mary Archer* wreck scheme. An' you know what Peterson says of him—didn't give him no trouble at all. One o' my best men, boys."

"There have been," observed Strokher stolidly, "certain stories told about Nickerson. Not that *I* wish to seem suspicious, but I put it to you as man to man."

"Ay," exclaimed Ally Bazan. "He was fair nutty once, they tell me. Threw some kind o' bally fit an' come aout all skew-jee'd in his mind. Forgot his nyme an' all. I s'y, how abaout him, anyw'y?"

"Boys," said Ryder, "I'll tell you. Nickerson—yes, I know the yarns about him. It was this way—y'see, I ain't keeping anything from you, boys. Two years ago he was a Methody preacher in Santa Clara. Well, he was what they call a revivalist, and he was holding forth one blazin' hot day out in the sun when all to once he goes down, *flat,* an' don't come round for the better part o' two days. When he wakes up he's *another person*; he'd forgot his name, forgot his job, forgot the whole blamed shooting match. *And he ain't never remembered them since.* The doctors have names for that kind o' thing. It seems it does happen now and again. Well, he turned to an' began sailoring first off—soon as the hospitals and medicos were done with him—an' him not having any friends as you might say, he was let go his own gait. He got to be third mate of some kind o' dough-dish down Mexico way; and then I got hold o' him an' took him into the Comp'ny. He's been with me ever since. He ain't got the faintest kind o' recollection o' his Methody days, an' believes he's always been a sailorman. Well, that's *his* business, ain't it? If he takes my orders an' walks chalk, what do I care about his Methody game? There, boys, is the origin, history and development of Slick Dick Nickerson. If you take up this sea-otter deal and go to Point Barrow, naturally Nick has got to go as owner's agent and representative of the Comp'ny. But I couldn't send an easier fellow to get along with. Honest, now, I couldn't. Boys, you think over the proposition between now and tomorrow an' then come around and let me know."

And the upshot of the whole matter was that one month later the *Bertha Millner,* with Nickerson, Hardenberg, Strokher and Ally Bazan on board, cleared from San Francisco, bound—the papers were beautifully precise—for Seattle and Tacoma with a cargo of general merchandise.

As a matter of fact, the bulk of her cargo consisted of some odd hundreds of very fine lumps of rock—which as ballast is cheap by the ton—and some odd dozen cases of conspicuously labeled champagne.

The Pacific and Oriental Flotation Company made this champagne out of Rhine wine, effervescent salts, raisins, rock candy and alcohol. It was from the same stock of wine of which Ryder had sold some thousand cases to the Koreans the year before.

II

"Not that I care a curse," said Strokher, the Englishman. "But I put it to you squarely that this voyage lacks that certain indescribable charm."

The *Bertha Millner* was a fortnight out, and the four adventurers—or, rather, the three adventurers and Nickerson—were lame in every joint, red-eyed from lack of sleep, half-starved, wholly wet and unequivocally disgusted. They had had heavy weather from the day they bade farewell to the whistling buoy off San Francisco Bay until the moment when even patient, docile, taciturn Strokher had at last—in his own fashion—rebelled.

"Ain't I a dam' fool? Ain't I a proper lot? Gard strike me if I don't chuck fer fair after this. Wot'd I come to sea fer—an' this 'ere go is the worst I *ever* knew—a baoat no bigger'n a bally bathtub, head seas, livin' gyles the clock 'round, wet food, wet clothes, wet bunks. Caold till, by crickey! I've lost the feel o' mee feet. An' wat for? For the bloomin' good chanst o' a slug in mee guts. That's wat for."

At little intervals the little vociferous colonial, Ally Bazan—he was red-haired and speckled—capered with rage, shaking his fists.

But Hardenberg only shifted his cigar to the other corner of his mouth. He knew Ally Bazan, and knew that the little fellow would have jeered at the offer of a first-cabin passage back to San Francisco in the swiftest, surest, steadiest passenger steamer that ever wore paint. So he remarked: "I ain't ever billed this promenade as a Coney Island picnic, I guess."

Nickerson—Slick Dick, the supercargo—was all that Hardenberg, who captained the schooner, could expect. He never interfered, never questioned; never protested in the name or interests of the Company when Hardenberg "hung on" in the bleak, bitter squalls till the *Bertha* was rail under and the sails hard as iron.

If it was true that he had once been a Methody revivalist no one, to quote Ally Bazan, "could 'a' smelled it off'n him." He was a black-bearded, scrawling six-footer, with a voice like a steam siren and a fist like a sledge. He carried two revolvers, spoke of the Russians at Point Barrow as the "Boomskys," and boasted if it came to *that* he'd engage to account for two of them, would shove their heads into their bootlegs and give them the running scrag, by God so he would!

Slowly, laboriously, beset in blinding fogs, swept with icy rains, buffeted and mauled and manhandled by the unending assaults of the sea, the *Bertha Millner* worked her way northward up that iron coast—till suddenly she entered an elysium.

Overnight she seemed to have run into it: it was a world of green, wooded islands, of smooth channels, of warm and steady winds, of cloudless skies. Coming on deck upon the morning of the *Bertha's* first day in this new region, Ally Bazan gazed open-mouthed. Then: "I s'y!" he yelled. "Hey! By crickey! Look!" He slapped his thighs. "S'trewth! This is 'eavenly."

Strokher was smoking his pipe on the hatch combings. "Rather," he observed. "An' I put it to you—we've deserved it."

In the main, however, the northward flitting was uneventful. Every fifth day Nickerson got drunk—on the Company's Korean champagne. Now that the weather had sweetened, the Three Black Crows had less to do in the way of handling and nursing the schooner. Their plans when the "Boomskys" should be reached were rehearsed over and over again. Then came spells of card and checker playing, storytelling, or hours of silent inertia when, man-fashion, they brooded over pipes in a patch of sun, somnolent, the mind empty of all thought.

But at length the air took on a keener tang; there was a bite to the breeze, the sun lost his savor and the light of him lengthened till Hardenberg could read off logarithms at ten in the evening. Greatcoats and sweaters were had from the chests, and it was no man's work to reef when the wind came down from out the north.

Each day now the schooner was drawing nearer the Arctic Circle. At length snow fell, and two days later they saw their first iceberg.

Hardenberg worked out their position on the chart and bore to the eastward till he made out the Alaskan coast—a smudge on the horizon. For another week he kept this in sight, the schooner dodging the bergs that by now drove by in squadrons, and even bumping and butling through drift and slush ice.

Seals were plentiful, and Hardenberg and Strokher promptly revived the quarrel of their respective nations. Once even they slew a mammoth bull walrus—astray from some northern herd— and played poker for the tusks. Then suddenly they pulled themselves sharply together, and, as it were, stood "attention." For more than a week the schooner, following the trend of the far-distant coast, had headed eastward, and now at length, looming out of the snow and out of the mist, a somber bulwark, black, vast, ominous, rose the scarps and crags of that which they came so far to see—Point Barrow.

Hardenberg rounded the point, ran in under the lee of the land and brought out the chart which Ryder had given him. Then he shortened sail and moved west again till Barrow was "hull down" behind him. To the north was the Arctic, treacherous, nursing hurricanes, ice-sheathed; but close aboard, not a quarter of a mile off his counter, stretched a gray and gloomy land, barren, bleak as a dead planet, inhospitable as the moon.

For three days they crawled along the edge keeping their glasses trained upon every bay, every inlet. Then at length, early one morning, Ally Bazan, who had been posted at the bows, came scrambling aft to Hardenberg at the wheel. He was gasping for breath in his excitement.

"Hi! There we are," he shouted. "O Lord! Oh, I s'y! Now we're in fer it. That's them! That's them! By the great jumpin' jimminy Christmas, that's them fer fair! Strike me blind for a bleedin' gutter cat if it eyent. O Lord! S'y, I gotta to get drunk. S'y, what all's the first jump in the bally game now?"

"Well, the first thing, little man," observed Hardenberg, "is for your mother's son to hang the monkey onto the safety valve. Keep y'r steam and watch y'r uncle."

"Scrag the Boomskys," said Slick Dick encouragingly.

Strokher pulled the left end of his viking mustache with the fingers of his right hand.

"We must now talk," he said.

A last conference was held in the cabin, and the various parts of the comedy rehearsed. Also the three looked to their revolvers.

"Not that I expect a rupture of diplomatic relations," commented Strokher; "but if there's any shooting done, as between man and man, I choose to do it."

"All understood, then?" asked Hardenberg, looking from face to face. "There won't be no chance to ask questions once we set foot ashore."

The others nodded.

It was not difficult to get in with the seven Russian sea-otter fishermen at the post. Certain of them spoke a macerated English, and through these Hardenberg, Ally Bazan and Nickerson—Strokher remained on board to look after the schooner—told to the "Boomskys" a lamentable tale of the reported wreck of a vessel, described by Hardenberg, with laborious precision, as a steam whaler from San Francisco—the *Tiber* by name, bark-rigged, seven hundred tons burden, Captain Henry Ward Beecher, mate Mr. James Boss Tweed. They, the visitors, were the officers of the relief ship on the lookout for castaways and survivors.

But in the course of these preliminaries it became necessary to restrain Nickerson—not yet wholly recovered from a recent incursion into the store of Korean champagne. It presented itself to his consideration as facetious to indulge (when speaking to the Russians) in strange and elaborate distortions of speech.

"And she sunk-avitch in a hundred fathom o' water-owski."

"—All on board-erewski."

"—Hell of dam' bad storm-onavna."

And he persisted in the idiocy till Hardenberg found an excuse for taking him aside and cursing him into a realization of his position.

In the end—inevitably—the schooner's company were invited to dine at the post.

It was a strange affair—a strange scene. The coast, flat, gray, dreary beyond all power of expression, lonesome as the interstellar space, and quite as cold, and in all that limitless vastness of the World's Edge, two specks—the hut, its three windows streaming with light, and the tiny schooner rocking in the offing. Over all flared the pallid incandescence of the auroras.

The company drank steadily, and Strokher, listening from the schooner's quarterdeck, heard the shouting and the songs faintly above the wash and lapping under the counter. Two hours had passed since the moment he guessed that the feast had been laid.

A third went by. He grew uneasy. There was no cessation of the noise of carousing. He even fancied he heard pistol shots. Then after a long time the noise by degrees wore down; a long silence followed. The hut seemed deserted; nothing stirred; another hour went by.

Then at length Strokher saw a figure emerge from the door of the hut and come down to the shore. It was Hardenberg. Strokher saw him wave his arm slowly, now to the left, now to the right, and he took down the wigwag as follows: "Stand—in—closer—we—have—the—skins."

III

During the course of the next few days Strokher heard the different versions of the affair in the hut over and over again till he knew its smallest details. He learned how the "Boomskys" fell upon Ryder's champagne like wolves upon a wounded buck, how they drank it from "enamelware" coffee cups, from tin dippers, from the bottles themselves; how at last they even dispensed with the tedium of removing the corks and knocked off the heads against the table ledge and drank from the splintered bottoms; how they quarreled over the lees and dregs, how ever and always fresh supplies were forthcoming, and how at last Hardenberg, Ally Bazan and Slick Dick stood up from the table in the midst of the seven inert bodies; how they ransacked the place for the priceless furs; how they failed to locate them; how the conviction grew that this was the wrong place after all, and how at length Hardenberg discovered the trapdoor that admitted to the cellar, where in the dim light of the uplifted lanterns they saw, corded in tiny bales and packages, the costliest furs known to commerce.

Ally Bazan had sobbed in his excitement over that vision and did not regain the power of articulate speech till the "loot" was safely stowed in the 'tween-decks and Hardenberg had given order to come about.

"Now," he had observed dryly, "now, lads, it's Hong Kong—or bust."

The tackle had fouled aloft and the jib hung slatting over the sprit like a collapsed balloon.

"Cast off up there, Nick!" called Hardenberg from the wheel.

Nickerson swung himself into the rigging, crying out in a mincing voice as, holding to a rope's end, he swung around to face the receding hut: "Bye-bye-skevitch. We've had *such* a charming evening. *Do* hope-sky we'll be able to come again-off." And as he spoke the lurch of the *Bertha* twitched his grip from the rope. He fell some thirty feet to the deck, and his head caromed against an iron cleat with a resounding crack.

"Here's luck," observed Hardenberg, twelve hours later, when Slick Dick, sitting on the edge of his bunk, looked stolidly and with fishy eyes from face to face. "We wa'n't quite shorthanded enough, it seems."

"Dotty for fair. Dotty for fair," exclaimed Ally Bazan; "clean off 'is nut. I s'y, Dick-ol'-chap, wyke-up, naow. Buck up. Buck up. 'Ave a drink."

But Nickerson could only nod his head and murmur: "A few more—consequently—and a good light——" Then his voice died down to unintelligible murmurs.

"We'll have to call at Juneau," decided Hardenberg two days later. " I don't figure on navigating this 'ere bathtub to no Hong Kong whatsoever, with three hands. We gotta pick up a couple o' A. B.'s in Juneau, if so be we can."

"How about the loot?" objected Strokher. "If one of those hands gets between decks he might smell—a sea otter, now. I put it to you he might."

"My son," said Hardenberg, "I've handled A. B.'s before"; and that settled the question.

During the first part of the run down, Nickerson gloomed silently over the schooner, looking curiously about him, now at his comrades' faces, now at the tumbling gray-green seas, now—and this by the hour—at his own hands. He seemed perplexed, dazed, trying very hard to get his bearings. But by and by he appeared, little by little, to come to himself. One day he pointed to the rigging with an unsteady forefinger, then, laying the same finger doubtfully upon his lips, said to Strokher: "A ship?"

"Quite so, quite so, me boy."

"Yes," muttered Nickerson absently, "a ship—of course."

Hardenberg expected to make Juneau on a Thursday. Wednesday afternoon Slick Dick came to him. He seemed never more master of himself. "How did I come aboard?" he asked.

Hardenberg explained.

"What have we been doing?"

"Why, don't you remember?" continued Hardenberg. He outlined the voyage in detail. "Then you remember," he went on, "we got up there to Point Barrow and found where the Russian fellows had their post, where they caught sea otters, and we went ashore and got 'em all full and lifted all the skins they had——"

"'Lifted'? You mean *stole* them."

"Come here," said the other. Encouraged by Nickerson's apparent convalescence, Hardenberg decided that the concrete evidence of things done would prove effective. He led him down into the 'tween-decks. "See now," he said. "See this packing case"—he pried up a board—"see these 'ere skins. Take one in y'r hand. Remember how we found 'em all in the cellar and hyked 'em out while the beggars slept?"

"Stole them? You say we got—that is *you* did—got somebody intoxicated and stole their property, and now you are on your way to dispose of it."

"Oh, well, if you want to put it thataway. Sure we did."

"I understand—— Well—— Let's go back on deck. I want to think this out."

The *Bertha Millner* crept into the harbor of Juneau in a fog, with ships' bells tolling on every side, let go her anchor at last in desperation and lay up to wait for the lifting. When this came the Three Crows looked at one another wide-eyed. They made out the drenched town and the dripping hills behind it. The quays, the custom house, the one hotel, and the few ships in the harbor. There were a couple of whalers from 'Frisco, a white, showily painted passenger boat from the same port, a Norwegian bark, and a freighter from Seattle grimy with coal dust. These, however, the *Bertha's* company ignored. Another boat claimed all their attention. In the fog they had let go not a pistol shot from her anchorage. She lay practically beside them. She was the United States revenue cutter *Bear*.

"But so long as they can't *smell* sea-otter skin," remarked Hardenberg, "I don't know that we're any the worse."

"All the syme," observed Ally Bazan, "I don't want to lose no bloomin' tyme a-pecking up aour bloomin' A. B.'s."

"I'll stay aboard and tend the baby," said Hardenberg with a wink. "You two move along ashore and get what you can—Scoovies for choice. Take Slick Dick with you. I reckon a change o' air might buck him up."

When the three had gone, Hardenberg, after writing up the painfully doctored log, set to work to finish a task on which the adventurers had been engaged in their leisure moments since leaving Point Barrow. This was the counting and sorting of the skins. The packing case had been broken open, and the scanty but precious contents littered an improvised table in the hold. Pen in hand, Hardenberg counted and ciphered and counted again. He could not forbear a chuckle when the net result was reached. The lot of the skins—the pelt of the sea otter is ridiculously small in proportion to its value—was no heavy load for the average man. But Hardenberg knew that once the "loot" was safely landed at the Hong Kong pierhead the Three Crows would share between them close upon ten thousand dollars. Even—if they had luck, and could dispose of the skins singly or in small lots—that figure might be doubled.

"And I call it a neat turn," observed Hardenberg. He was aroused by the noise of hurried feet upon the deck, and there was that in their sound that brought him upright in a second, hand on hip. Then, after a second, he jumped out on deck to meet Ally Bazan and Strokher, who had just scrambled over the rail.

"Bust. B-u-s-t!" remarked the Englishman.

"'Ere's 'ell to pay," cried Ally Bazan in a hoarse whisper, glancing over at the revenue cutter.

"Where's Nickerson?" demanded Hardenberg.

"That's it," answered the colonial. "That's where it's 'ell. Listen naow. He goes ashore along o' us, quiet and peaceable like, never battin' a' eye, we givin' him a bit o' jolly, y' know, to keep him chirked up as ye might s'y. But so soon as ever he sets foot on shore, abaout faice he gaoes, plumb into the Custom's orfice. I s'ys, 'Wot all naow, messmite? Come along aout o' that.' But he turns on me like a bloomin' babby an' s'ys he: 'Hands orf, wretch!' Ay, them's just his words. Just like that, 'Hands orf, wretch!' And then he nips into the orfice an' marches fair up to the desk an' s'ys like this—we heerd him, havin' followed on to the door—he s'ys, just like this:

"'Orfficer, I am a min'ster o' the gospel, o' the Methodis' denomineyetion, an' I'm deteyined agin my will along o' a pirate ship which has robbed certain parties o' val-able goods. Which syme I'm pre-pared to attest afore a no'try publick, an' lodge informeye-tion o' crime. An', s'ys he, 'I demand the protection o' the authorities an' arsk to be directed to the American consul.'

"S'y, we never wyted to hear no more, but hyked awye hot foot. S'y, wot all now. Oh, mee Gord! eyen't it a rum gao for fair? S'y, let's get aout o' here, Hardy, dear."

"Look there," said Hardenberg, jerking his head toward the cutter, "how far'd we get before the customs would 'a' passed the tip to *her* and she'd started to overhaul us? That's what they feed her for—to round up the likes o' us."

"We got to do something rather soon," put in Strokher. "Here comes the custom house dinghy now."

As a matter of fact, a boat was putting off from the dock. At her stern fluttered the custom-house flag.

"Bitched—bitched for fair!" cried Ally Bazan.

"Quick, now!" exclaimed Hardenberg. "On the jump! Overboard with that loot!—or no. Steady! That won't do. There's that dam' cutter. They'd see it go. Here!—into the galley. There's a fire in the stove. Get a move on!"

"Wot!" wailed Ally Bazan. "Burn the little joker? Gord, I *can't*, Hardy, I *can't*. It's agin human nature."

"You can do time in San Quentin, then, for felony," retorted Strokher as he and Hardenberg dashed by him, their arms full of the skins. "You can do time in San Quentin else. Make your choice. I put it to you as between man and man."

With set teeth, and ever and again glancing over the rail at the oncoming boat, the two fed their fortune to the fire. The pelts, partially cured and still fatty, blazed like crude oil, the hair crisping, the hides melting into rivulets of grease. For a minute the schooner reeked of the smell and a stifling smoke poured from the galley stack. Then the embers of the fire guttered and a long whiff of sea wind blew away the reek. A single skin, fallen in the scramble, still remained on the floor of the galley. Hardenberg snatched it up, tossed it into the flames and clapped the door to.

"Now, let him squeal," he declared. "You fellows, when that boat gets here, let *me* talk; keep your mouths shut or, by God, we'll all wear stripes."

The Three Crows watched the boat's approach in a silence broken only once by a long whimper from Ally Bazan. "An' it was a-workin' out as lovely as Billy-oh," he said, "till that syme underbred costermonger's swipe remembered he was Methody—an' him who, only a few d'ys back, went raound s'yin' 'scrag the "Boomskys"!' A couple o' thousand pounds gone as quick as look at it. Oh, I eyn't never goin' to git over this."

The boat came up and the Three Crows were puzzled to note that no brass-buttoned personage sat in the stern sheets, no harbor police glowered at them from the bow, no officer of the law fixed them with the eye of suspicion. The boat was manned only by a couple of freight handlers in woolen Jerseys, upon the breasts of which were affixed the two letters, "C. H."

"Say," called one of the freight handlers, "is this the *Bertha Millner?*"

"Yes," answered Hardenberg, his voice at a growl. "An' what might you want with her, my friend?"

"Well, look here," said the other, "one of your hands came ashore mad as a coot and broke into the house of the American Consul, and resisted arrest and raised hell generally. The inspector says you got to send a provost guard or something ashore to take him off. There's been several mix-ups among ships' crews lately and the town——"

The tide drifted the boat out of hearing, and Hardenberg sat down on the capstan head, turning his back to his comrades. There was a long silence. Then he said:

"Boys, let's go home. I—I want to have a talk with President Ryder."

DYING FIRES

Young Overbeck's father was editor and proprietor of the county paper in Colfax, California, and the son, so soon as his high school days were over, made his appearance in the office as his father's assistant. So abrupt was the transition that his diploma, which was to hang over the editorial desk, had not yet returned from the framer's, while the first copy that he was called on to edit was his own commencement oration on the philosophy of Dante. He had worn a white piqué cravat and a cutaway coat on the occasion of its delivery, and the county commissioner, who was the guest of honor on the platform, had congratulated him as he handed him his sheepskin. For Overbeck was the youngest and the brightest member of his class.

Colfax was a lively town in those days. The teaming from the valley over into the mining country on the other side of the Indian River was at its height then. Colfax was the headquarters of the business, and the teamsters—after the long pull up from the Indian River Canyon—showed interest in an environment made up chiefly of saloons.

Then there were the mining camps over by Iowa Hill, the Morning Star, the Big Dipper, and farther on, up in the Gold Run country, the Little Providence. There was Dutch Flat, full of Mexican-Spanish girls and "breed" girls, where the dance halls were of equal number with the bars. There was—a little way down the line—Clipper Gap, where the mountain ranches began, and where the mountain cowboy lived up to the traditions of his kind.

And this life, tumultuous, headstrong, vivid in color, vigorous in action, was bound together by the railroad, which not only made a single community out of all that part of the east slope of the Sierras' foothills, but contributed its own life as well—the life of oilers, engineers, switchmen, eating-house waitresses and cashiers, "lady" operators, conductors, and the like.

Of such a little world news items are evolved—sometimes even scarehead, double-leaded descriptive articles—supplemented by interviews with sheriffs and antemortem statements. Good grist for a county paper; good opportunities for an unspoiled, observant, imaginative young fellow at the formative period of his life. Such was the time, such the environment, such the conditions that prevailed when young Overbeck, at the age of twenty-one, sat down to the writing of his first novel.

He completed it in five months, and, though he did not know the fact then, the novel was good. It was not great—far from it, but it was not merely clever. Somehow, by a miracle of good fortune, young Overbeck had got started right at the very beginning. He had not been influenced by a fetish of his choice till his work was a mere replica of some other writer's. He was not literary. He had not much time for books. He lived in the midst of a strenuous, eager life, a little primal even yet; a life of passions that were often elemental in their simplicity and directness. His schooling and his newspaper work—it was he who must find or ferret out the news all along the line, from Penrhyn to Emigrant Gap—had taught him observation without—here was the miracle—dulling the edge of his sensitiveness. He saw, as those few, few people see who live close to life at the beginning of an epoch. He saw into the life and the heart beneath the life; the life and the heart of Bunt McBride, as with eight horses and much abjuration he negotiated a load of steel "stamps" up the sheer leap of the Indian Canyon; he saw into the life and into the heart of Irma Tejada, who kept case for the faro players at Dutch Flat; he saw into the life and heart of Lizzie Toby, the biscuit shooter in the railway eating-house, and into the life and heart of "Doc" Twitchel, who had degrees from Edinburgh and Leipzig, and who, for obscure reasons, chose to look after the measles, sprains, and rheumatisms of the countryside.

And, besides, there were others and still others, whom young Overbeck learned to know to the very heart of them: blacksmiths, traveling peddlers, section bosses, miners, horse wranglers, cowpunchers, the stage drivers, the storekeeper, the hotel keeper, the ditch tender, the prospector, the seamstress of the town, the postmistress, the schoolmistress, the poetess. Into the lives of these and the hearts of these young Overbeck saw, and the wonder of that sight so overpowered him that he had no thought and no care for other people's books. And he was only twenty-one! Only twenty-one, and yet he saw clearly into the great, complicated, confused human machine that clashed and jarred around him. Only twenty-one, and yet he read the enigma that men of fifty may alone hope to solve! Once in a great while this thing may happen—in such out-of-the-way places as that country around Colfax in Placer County, California, where no outside influences have play, where books are few and misprized and the reading circle a thing unknown. From time to time such men are born, especially along the line of cleavage where the farthest skirmish line of civilization thrusts and girds at the wilderness. A very few find their true profession before the fire is stamped out of them; of these few, fewer still have the force to make themselves heard. Of these last the majority die before they attain the faculty of making their message intelligible. Those that remain are the world's great men.

At the time when his first little book was on its initial journey to the Eastern publishing houses, Overbeck was by no means a great man. The immaturity that was yet his, the lack of knowledge of his tools, clogged his work and befogged his vision. The smooth running of the cogs and the far-darting range of vision would come in the course of the next fifteen years of unrelenting persistence. The ordering and organizing and controlling of his machine he could, with patience and by taking thought, accomplish for himself. The original impetus had come straight from the almighty gods. That impetus was young yet, feeble yet, coming down from so far it was spent by the time it reached the earth—at Colfax, California. A touch now might divert it. Judge with what care such a thing should be nursed and watched; compared with the delicacy with which it unfolds, the opening of a rosebud is an abrupt explosion. Later on, such insight, such undeveloped genius may become a tremendous world power, a thing to split a nation in twain as the ax cleaves the block. But at twenty-one, a whisper—and it takes flight; a touch—it withers; the lifting of a finger—it is gone.

The same destiny that had allowed Overbeck to be born, and that thus far had watched over his course, must have inspired his choice, his very first choice, of a publisher, for the manuscript of *The Vision of Bunt McBride* went straight as a homebound bird to the one man of all others who could understand the beginnings of genius and recognize the golden grain of truth in the chaff of unessentials. His name was Conant, and he accepted the manuscript by telegram.

He did more than this, and one evening Overbeck stood on the steps of the post office and opened a letter in his hand, and, looking up and off, saw the world transfigured. His chance had come. In half a year of time he had accomplished what other men—other young writers—strive for throughout the best years of their youth. He had been called to New York. Conant had offered him a minor place on his editorial staff.

Overbeck reached the great city a fortnight later, and the cutaway coat and piqué cravat—unworn since Commencement—served to fortify his courage at the first interview with the man who was to make him—so he believed—famous.

Ah, the delights, the excitement, the inspiration of that day! Let those judge who have striven toward the Great City through years of deferred hope and heart sinkings and sacrifice daily renewed. Overbeck's feet were set in those streets whose names had become legendary to his imagination. Public buildings and public squares familiar only through the weekly prints defiled before him like a pageant, but friendly for all that, inviting even. But the vast conglomerate life that roared by his ears, like the systole and diastole of an almighty heart, was for a moment disquieting. Soon the human resemblance faded. It became as a machine infinitely huge, infinitely formidable. It challenged him with superb condescension.

"I must down you," he muttered, as he made his way toward Conant's, "or you will down me." He saw it clearly. There was no other alternative. The young boy in his foolish finery of a Colfax tailor's make, with no weapons but such wits as the gods had given him, was pitted against the leviathan.

There was no friend nearer than his native state on the other fringe of the continent. He was fearfully alone.

But he was twenty-one. The wits that the gods had given him were good, and the fine fire that was within him, the radiant freshness of his nature, stirred and leaped to life at the challenge. Ah, he would win, he would win! And in his exuberance, the first dim consciousness of his power came to him. He could win, he had it in him; he began to see that now. That nameless power was his which would enable him to grip this monstrous life by the very throat, and bring it down on its knee before him to listen respectfully to what he had to say.

The interview with Conant was no less exhilarating. It was in the reception room of the great house that it took place, and while waiting for Conant to come in, Overbeck, his heart in his mouth, recognized, in the original drawings on the walls, picture after picture, signed by famous illustrators, that he had seen reproduced in Conant's magazine.

Then Conant himself had appeared and shaken the young author's hand a long time, and had talked to him with the utmost kindness of his book, of his plans for the immediate future, of the work he would do in the editorial office and of the next novel he wished him to write.

"We'll only need you here in the mornings," said the editor, "and you can put in your afternoons on your novel. Have you anything in mind as good as *Bunt McBride*?"

"I have a sort of notion for one," hazarded the young man; and Conant had demanded to hear it.

Stammering, embarrassed, Overbeck outlined it.

"I see, I see!" Conant commented. "Yes, there is a good story in that. Maybe Hastings will want to use it in the monthly. But we'll make a book of it, anyway, if you work it up as well as the McBride story."

And so the young fellow made his first step in New York. The very next day he began his second novel.

In the editorial office, where he spent his mornings reading proof and making up "front matter," he made the acquaintance of a middle-aged lady, named Miss Patten, who asked him to call on her, and later on introduced him into the "set" wherein she herself moved. The set called itself the "New Bohemians," and once a week met at Miss Patten's apartment uptown. In a month's time Overbeck was a fixture in "New Bohemia."

It was made up of minor poets whose opportunity in life was the blank space on a magazine page below the end of an article; of men past their prime, who, because of an occasional story in a second-rate monthly, were considered to have "arrived"; of women who translated novels from the Italian and Hungarian; of decayed dramatists who could advance unimpeachable reasons for the non-production of their plays; of novelists whose books were declined by publishers because of professional jealousy on the part of the "readers," or whose ideas, stolen by false friends, had appeared in books that sold by the hundreds of thousands. In public the New Bohemians were fulsome in the praise of one another's productions. Did a sonnet called, perhaps, "A Cryptogram Is Stella's Soul" appear in a current issue, they fell on it with eager eyes, learned it by heart and recited lines of it aloud; the conceit of the lover translating the cipher by the key of love was welcomed with transports of delight.

"Ah, one of the most exquisitely delicate allegories I've ever heard, and so true—so 'in the tone'!"

Did a certain one of the third-rate novelists, reading aloud from his unpublished manuscript, say of his heroine: "It was the native catholicity of his temperament that lent strength and depth to her innate womanliness," the phrase was snapped up on the instant.

"How he understands women!"

"Such *finesse!* More subtle than Henry James."

"Paul Bourget has gone no further," said one of the critics of New Bohemia; "our limitations are determined less by our renunciations than by our sense of proportion in our conception of ethical standards."

The set abased itself. "Wonderful, ah, how pitilessly you fathom our poor human nature!" New Bohemia saw color in word effects. A poet read aloud:

> "The stalwart rain!
> Ah, the rush of down-toppling waters;
> The torrent!
> Merge of mist and musky air;
> The current
> Sweeps thwart my blinded sight again."

"Ah!" exclaimed one of the audience, "see, see that bright green flash!"

Thus in public. In private all was different. Walking home with one or another of the set, young Overbeck heard their confidences.

"Keppler is a good fellow right enough, but, my goodness, he can't write verse!"

"That thing of Miss Patten's tonight! Did you ever hear anything so unconvincing, so obvious? Poor old woman!"

"I'm really sorry for Martens; awfully decent sort, but he never should try to write novels."

By rapid degrees young Overbeck caught the lingo of the third-raters. He could talk about "tendencies" and the "influence of reactions." Such and such a writer had a "sense of form," another a "feeling for word effects." He knew all about "tones" and "notes" and "philistinisms." He could tell the difference between an allegory and a simile as far as he could see them. An anticlimax was the one unforgivable sin under heaven. A mixed metaphor made him wince, and a split infinitive hurt him like a blow.

But the great word was "convincing." To say a book was convincing was to give positively the last verdict. To be "unconvincing" was to be shut out from the elect. If the New Bohemian decided that the last popular book was unconvincing, there was no appeal. The book was not to be mentioned in polite conversation.

And the author of *The Vision of Bunt McBride*, as yet new to the world as the day he was born, with all his eager ambition and quick sensitiveness, thought that all this was the real thing. He had never so much as seen literary people before. How could he know the difference? He honestly believed that New Bohemia was the true literary force of New York. He wrote home that the association with such people, thinkers, poets, philosophers, was an inspiration; that he had learned more in one week in their company than he had learned in Colfax in a whole year.

Perhaps, too, it was the flattery he received that helped to carry Overbeck off his feet. The New Bohemians made a little lion of him when *Bunt McBride* reached its modest pinnacle of popularity. They kowtowed to him, and toadied to him, and fagged and tooted for him, and spoke of his book as a masterpiece. They said he had succeeded where Kipling had ignominiously failed. They said there was more harmony of prose effects in one chapter of *Bunt McBride* than in everything that Bret Harte ever wrote.

They told him he was a second Stevenson—only with more refinement.

Then the women of the set, who were of those who did not write, who called themselves "mere dilettantes," but who "took an interest in young writers" and liked to influence their lives and works, began to flutter and buzz around him. They told him that they understood him; that they understood his temperament; that they could see where his forte lay; and they undertook his education.

There was in *The Vision of Bunt McBride* a certain sane and healthy animalism that hurt nobody, and that, no doubt, Overbeck, in later books, would modify. He had taken life as he found it to make his book; it was not his fault that the teamsters, biscuit shooters, and "breed" girls of the foothills were coarse in fiber. In his sincerity he could not do otherwise in his novel than paint life as he saw it. He had dealt with it honestly; he did not dab at the edge of the business; he had sent his fist straight through it.

But the New Bohemians could not abide this.

"Not so much *faroucherie*, you dear young Lochinvar!" they said. "Art must uplift. 'Look thou not down, but up toward uses of a cup';" and they supplemented the quotation by lines from Walter Pater, and read to him from Ruskin and Matthew Arnold.

Ah, the spiritual was the great thing. We were here to make the world brighter and better for having lived in it. The passions of a waitress in a railway eating-house—how sordid the subject. Dear boy, look for the soul, strive to rise to higher planes! Tread upward; every book should leave a clean taste in the mouth, should tend to make one happier, should elevate, not debase.

So by degrees Overbeck began to see his future in a different light. He began to think that he really had succeeded where Kipling had failed; that he really was Stevenson with more refinement, and that the one and only thing lacking in his work was soul. He believed that he must strive for the spiritual, and "let the ape and tiger die." The originality and unconventionality of his little book he came to regard as crudities.

"Yes," he said one day to Miss Patten and a couple of his friends, "I have been rereading my book of late. I can see its limitations—now. It has a lack of form; the tonality is a little false. It fails somehow to convince."

Thus the first winter passed. In the mornings Overbeck assiduously edited copy and made up front matter on the top floor of the Conant building. In the evenings he called on Miss Patten, or some other member of the set. Once a week, uptown, he fed fat on the literary delicatessen that New Bohemia provided. In the meantime, every afternoon, from luncheon time till dark, he toiled on his second novel, *Renunciations*. The environment of *Renunciations* was a far cry from Colfax, California. It was a city-bred story, with no fresher atmosphere than that of bought flowers. Its *dramatis personae* were all of the leisure class, operagoers, intriguers, riders of blood horses, certainly more refined than Lizzie Toby, biscuit shooter, certainly more *spirituelle* than Irma Tejada, case keeper in Dog Omahone's faro joint, certainly more elegant than Bunt McBride, teamster of the Colfax Iowa Hill Freight Transportation Company.

From time to time, as the novel progressed, he read it to the dilettante women whom he knew best among the New Bohemians. They advised him as to its development, and "influenced" its outcome and dénouement.

"I think you have found your *métier*, dear boy," said one of them, when *Renunciations* was nearly completed. "To portray the concrete—is it not a small achievement, sublimated journalese, nothing more? But to grasp abstractions, to analyze a woman's soul, to evoke the spiritual essence in humanity, as you have done in your ninth chapter of *Renunciations*—that is the true function of art. *Je vous fais mes compliments. Renunciations* is a *chef-d'oeuvre*. Can't you see yourself what a stride you have made, how much broader your outlook has become, how much more catholic, since the days of *Bunt McBride*?"

To be sure, Overbeck could see it. Ah, he was growing, he was expanding. He was mounting higher planes. He was more—catholic. That, of all words, was the one to express his mood. Catholic, ah, yes, he was catholic!

When *Renunciations* was finished he took the manuscript to Conant and waited a fortnight in an agony of suspense and repressed jubilation for the great man's verdict. He was all the more anxious to hear it because, every now and then, while writing the story, doubts—distressing, perplexing—had intruded. At times and all of a sudden, after days of the steadiest footing, the surest progress, the story—the whole set and trend of the affair—

would seem, as it were, to escape from his control. Where once, in *Bunt McBride,* he had gripped, he must now grope. What was it? He had been so sure of himself, with all the stimulus of new surroundings, the work in this second novel should have been all the easier. But the doubt would fade, and for weeks he would plough on, till again, and all unexpectedly, he would find himself in an agony of indecision as to the outcome of some vital pivotal episode of the story. Of two methods of treatment, both equally plausible, he could not say which was the true, which the false; and he must needs take, as it were, a leap in the dark—it was either that or abandoning the story, trusting to mere luck that he would, somehow, be carried through.

A fortnight after he had delivered the manuscript to Conant he presented himself in the publisher's office.

"I was just about to send for you," said Conant. "I finished your story last week."

There was a pause. Overbeck settled himself comfortably in his chair, but his nails were cutting his palms.

"Hastings has read it, too—and—well, frankly, Overbeck, we were disappointed."

"Yes?" inquired Overbeck calmly. "H'm—that's too b-bad."

He could not hear, or at least could not understand, just what the publisher said next. Then, after a time that seemed immeasurably long, he caught the words:

"It would not do you a bit of good, my boy, to have us publish it—it would harm you. There are a good many things I would lie about, but books are not included. This *Renunciations* of yours is—is, why, confound it, Overbeck, it's foolishness."

Overbeck went out and sat on a bench in a square nearby, looking vacantly at a fountain as it rose and fell and rose again with an incessant cadenced splashing. Then he took himself home to his hall bedroom. He had brought the manuscript of his novel with him, and for a long time he sat at his table listlessly turning the leaves, confused, stupid, all but inert. The end, however, did not come suddenly. A few weeks later *Renunciations* was published, but not by Conant. It bore the imprint of an obscure firm in Boston. The covers were of limp dressed leather, olive-green, and could be tied together by thongs, like a portfolio. The sale stopped after five hundred copies had been ordered, and the real critics, those who did not belong to New Bohemia, hardly so much as noticed the book.

In the autumn, when the third-raters had come back from their vacations, the "evenings" at Miss Patten's were resumed, and Overbeck hurried to the very first meeting. He wanted to talk it all over with them. In his chagrin and cruel disappointment he was hungry for some word of praise, of condolement. He wanted to be told again, even though he had begun to suspect many things, that he had succeeded where Kipling had failed, that he was Stevenson with more refinement.

But the New Bohemians, the same women and fakirs and half-baked minor poets who had "influenced" him and had ruined him, could hardly find time to notice him now. The guest of the evening was a new little lion who had joined the set. A symbolist versifier who wrote over the pseudonym of de la Houssaye, with black, oily hair and long, white hands; him the Bohemians thronged about in crowds as before they had thronged about Overbeck. Only once did any one of them pay attention to the latter. This was the woman who had nicknamed him "Young Lochinvar." Yes, she had read *Renunciations*, a capital little thing, a little thin in parts, lacking in *finesse.* He must strive for his true medium of expression, his true note. Ah, art was long! Study of the new symbolists would help him. She would beg him to read Monsieur de la Houssaye's *The Monoliths.* Such subtlety, such delicious word chords! It could not fail to inspire him.

Shouldered off, forgotten, the young fellow crept back to his little hall bedroom and sat down to think it over. There in the dark of the night his eyes were opened, and he saw, at last, what these people had done to him; saw the Great Mistake, and that he had wasted his substance.

The golden apples, that had been his for the stretching of the hand, he had flung from him. Tricked, trapped, exploited, he had prostituted the great good thing that had been his by right divine, for the privilege of eating husks with swine. Now was the day of the mighty famine, and the starved and broken heart of him, crying out for help, found only a farrago of empty phrases.

He tried to go back; he did, in very fact, go back to the mountains and the canyons of the great Sierras. "He arose and went to his father," and, with such sapped and broken strength as New

Bohemia had left him, strove to wrest some wreckage from the dying fire.

But the ashes were cold by now. The fire that the gods had allowed him to snatch, because he was humble and pure and clean and brave, had been stamped out beneath the feet of minor and dilettante poets, and now the gods guarded close the brands that yet remained on the altars.

They may not be violated twice, those sacred fires. Once in a lifetime the very young and the pure in heart may see the shine of them and pluck a brand from the altar's edge. But, once possessed, it must be watched with a greater vigilance than even that of the gods, for its light will live only for him who snatched it first. Only for him that shields it, even with his life, from the contact of the world does it burst into a burning and a shining light. Let once the touch of alien fingers disturb it, and there remains only a little heap of bitter ashes.

THE GUEST OF HONOR

PART ONE

The doctor shut and locked his desk drawer upon his memorandum book with his right hand, and extended the left to his friend Manning Verrill, with the remark:

"Well, Manning, how are you?"

"If I were well, Henry," answered Verrill gravely, "I would not be here."

The doctor leaned back in his deep leather chair, and having carefully adjusted his glasses, tilted back his head, and looked at Verrill from beneath them. He waited for him to continue.

"It's my nerves—I *suppose*," began Verrill. "Henry," he declared suddenly, leaning forward, "Henry, I'm scared; that's what's the matter with me—I'm scared."

"Scared?" echoed the doctor. "What nonsense! What of?"

"Scared of death, Henry," broke out Verrill, "scared *blue!*"

"It is your nerves," murmured the doctor. "You need travel and a bromide, my boy. There's nothing the matter with you. Why, you're good for another forty years—yes, or even for another fifty years. You're sound as a nut. You, to talk about death!"

"I've seen thirty—twenty-nine I should say, twenty-nine of my best friends go."

The doctor looked puzzled a moment; then—"Oh! you mean that club of yours," said he.

"Yes," said Verrill. "Great heavens! to think that I should be the last man, after all—well, one of us had to be the last. And that's where the trouble is, Henry. It's been growing on me for the last two years—ever since Curtice died. He was the twenty-sixth. And

137

he died only a month before the Annual Dinner. Arnold, Brill, Steve—Steve Sharrett you know, and I—just the four—were left then; and we sat down to that big table alone; and when we came to the toast of 'The Absent Ones'.... Well, Henry, we were pretty solemn before we got through. And we knew that the choice of the last man—who would face those thirty-one empty covers and open the bottle of wine that we all set aside at our first dinner, and drink 'The Absent Ones'—was narrowing down pretty fine.

"Next year there were only Arnold and Steve and myself left. Brill—well, you know all about his death. The three of us got through dinner somehow. The year after that we were still three, and even the year after that. Then poor old Steve went down with the *Dreibund* in the bay of Biscay, and four months afterward Arnold and I sat down to the table at the Annual, alone. I'm not going to forget that evening in a hurry. Why, Henry—oh! never mind. Then——"

"Well," prompted the doctor as his friend paused.

"Arnold died three months ago. And the day of our Annual—I mean my—the club's," Verrill changed his position. "The date of the dinner, the Annual Dinner, is next month, and I'm the only one left."

"And, of course, you'll not go," declared the doctor.

"Oh, yes," said Verrill. "Yes, I will go, of course. But——" He shook his head with a long sigh. "When the Last Man Club was organized," he went on, "in '68, we were all more or less young. It was a great idea, at least I felt that way about it, but I didn't believe that thirty young men would persist in anything—of that sort—very long. But no member of the club died for the first five years, and the club met every year and had its dinner without much thought of—of consequences, and of the inevitable. We met just to be sociable."

"Hold on," interrupted the doctor, "you are speaking now of thirty. A while ago you said thirty-one."

"Yes, I know," assented Verrill. "There were thirty in the club, but we always placed an extra cover—for—for the Guest of Honor."

The doctor made a movement of impatience. Then in a moment, "Well," he said resignedly, "go on."

"That's about the essentials," answered Verrill. "The first death was in '73. And from that year on the vacant places at the table have steadily increased. Little by little the original bravado of the thing dropped out of it all for me; and of late years—well, I have told you how it is. I've seen so many of them die, and die so fast, so regularly—one a year you might say—that I've kept saying 'who next, who next, who's to go this year?' . . . And as they went, one by one, and still I was left. . . . I tell you, Henry, the suspense was, . . . the suspense is. . . . You see I'm the last now, and ever since Curtice died, I've felt this thing weighing on me. *By God, Henry, I'm afraid; I'm afraid of Death! It's horrible!* It's as though I were on the list of 'condemned' and were listening to hear my name called every minute."

"Well, so are all of us, if you come to that," observed the doctor.

"Oh, I know, I know," cried Verrill, "it is morbid and all that. But that don't help *me* any. Can you imagine me one month from tomorrow night? Think now. I'm alone, absolutely, and there is the long, empty table, with the thirty places set, and the extra place, and those places are where all my old friends used to sit. And at twelve I get up and give first 'The Absent Ones,' and then 'The Guest of the Evening.' I gave those toasts last year, but there were two of us, then, and the year before there were three. But ever since Curtice died and we were narrowed down to four, this thing has been weighing on me—this idea of death, and I've conceived a horror of it—a—a dread. And now I am the last. I had no idea this would ever happen to me; or if it did, that it would be like this. I'm shaken, Henry, shaken. I've not slept for three nights. So I've come to you. You must help me."

"So I will, by advising you. You give up the idiocy. Cut out the dinner this year; yes, and for always."

"You don't understand," replied Verrill calmly. "It is impossible. I could not keep away. I *must* be there."

"But it's simple lunacy," expostulated the doctor. "Man, you've worked upon your nerves over this fool club and dinner, till I won't be responsible for you if you carry out this notion. Come, promise me you will take the train for, say, Florida, tomorrow, and *I'll* give you stuff that will make you sleep. St. Augustine is heaven at this time of year, and I hear the tarpon have come in. Shall——"

Verrill shook his head.

"You don't understand," he repeated. "You simply don't understand. No, I shall go to the dinner. But of course I'm—I'm nervous—a little. Did I say I was scared? I didn't mean that. Oh, I'm all right; I just want you to prescribe for me, something for the nerves. Henry, death is a terrible thing—to see 'em all struck down, twenty-nine of 'em—splendid boys. Henry, I'm not a coward. There's a difference between cowardice and fear. For hours last night I was trying to work it out. Cowardice—that's just turning tail and running; but I shall go through that Annual Dinner, and that's ordeal enough, believe me. But fear—it's just death in the abstract that unmans me. *That's* the thing to fear. To think that we all go along living and working and fussing from day to day, when we *know* that this great Monster, this Horror, is walking up and down the streets, and that sooner or later he'll catch us—that we can't escape. Isn't it the greatest curse in the world! We're so used to it we don't realize the Thing. But suppose one could eliminate the Monster altogether. *Then* we'd realize how sweet life was, and we'd look back at the old days with horror— just as I do now."

"Oh, but this is rubbish," cried the doctor, "simple drivel. Manning, I'm ashamed of you. I'll prescribe for you, I suppose I've got to. But a good rough fishing-and-hunting trip would do more for you than a gallon of drugs. If you won't go to Florida, get out of town, if it's only over Sunday. Here's your prescription, and *do* take a Friday-to-Monday trip. Tramp in the woods, get tired, and *don't go to that dinner!*"

"You don't understand," repeated Verrill, as the two stood up. He put the prescription into his pocketbook. "You don't understand. I couldn't keep away. It's a duty, and besides—well, I couldn't make you see. Good-bye. This stuff will make me sleep, eh? And do my nerves good, too, you say? I see. I'll come back to you if it don't work. Good-bye again. *This* door, is it? Not through the waiting room, eh? Yes, I remember.... Henry, did you ever— did you ever face death yourself—I mean——"

"Nonsense, nonsense, nonsense," cried the doctor. But Verrill persisted. His back to the closed door, he continued:

"*I* did. *I* faced death once, so you see I should know. It was when I was a lad of twenty. My father had a line of New Orleans packets and I often used to make the trip as supercargo. One October day we were caught in the equinox off Hatteras, and before we knew it we were wondering if she would last another half hour. Along in the afternoon there came a sea aboard, and caught me unawares. I lost my hold and felt myself going, going. ... I was sure for ten seconds that it was the end—*and I saw death then, face to face!*

"And I've never forgotten it. I've only to shut my eyes to see it all, hear it all—the naked spars rocking against the gray-blue of the sky, the wrench and creak of the ship, the threshing of rope ends, the wilderness of pale-green water, the sound of rain and scud.... No, no, I'll not forget it. And death was a horrid specter in that glimpse I got of him. I—I don't care to see him again. Well, good-bye once more."

"Good-bye, Manning, and believe me, this is all hypochondria. Go and catch fish. Go shoot something, and in twenty-four hours you'll believe there's no such thing as death."

The door closed. Verrill was gone.

PART TWO

The banquet hall was in the top story of one of the loftiest skyscrapers of the city. Along the eastern wall was a row of windows reaching from ceiling to floor, and as the extreme height of the building made it unnecessary to draw the curtains whoever was at the table could look out and over the entire city in that direction. Thus it was that Manning Verrill, on a certain night some four weeks after his interview with the doctor, sat there at his walnuts and black coffee and, absorbed, abstracted, looked out over the panorama beneath him, where the Life of a great nation centered and throbbed.

To the unenlightened the hall would have presented a strange spectacle. Down its center extended the long table. The chairs were drawn up, the covers laid. But the chairs were empty, the covers untouched; and but for the presence of the one man the hall was empty, deserted.

At the head of the table Verrill, in evening dress, a gardenia in his lapel, his napkin across his lap, an unlighted cigar in his fingers, sat motionless, looking out over the city with unseeing eyes. Of thirty places around the table, none was distinctive, none varied. But at Verrill's right hand the thirty-first place, the place of honor, differed from all the rest. The chair was large, massive. The oak of which it was made was black, while instead of the usual array of silver and porcelain, one saw but two vessels—an unopened bottle of wine and a large silver cup heavily chased.

From far below in the city's streets eleven o'clock struck. The sounds broke in upon Verrill's reverie and he stirred, glanced about the room and then, rising, went to the window and stood there for some time looking out.

At his feet, far beneath, lay the city, twinkling with lights. In the business quarter all was dark, but from the district of theaters and restaurants there arose a glare into the night, ruddy, vibrating, with here and there a ganglion of electric bulbs upon a "fire sign" emphasizing itself in a whiter radiance. Cable cars and cabs threaded the streets with little starring eyes of colored lights, while underneath all this blur of illumination, the people, debouching from the theaters, filled the sidewalks with tiny ant-like swarms, minute, bustling.

Farther on in the residence district, occasional lighted windows watched with the street lamps gazing blankly into the darkness. In particular one house was all ablaze. Every window glowed. No doubt a great festivity was in progress and Verrill could almost fancy that he heard the strains of the music, the rustle of the silks.

Then nearer at hand, but more to the eastward, where the office buildings rose in tower-like clusters and somber groups, Verrill could see a vista of open water—the harbor. Lights were moving here, green and red, as the great hoarse-voiced freighters stood out with the tide.

And beyond this was the sea itself, and more lights, very, very faint where the ships rolled leisurely in the ground swells; ships bound to and from all ports of the earth—ships that united the nations, that brought the whole world of living men under the view of the lonely watcher in the empty Banquet Hall.

Verrill raised the window. At once a subdued murmur, prolonged, monotonous—the same murmur as that which disengages itself from forests, from the sea, and from sleeping armies—rose to meet him. It was the mingling of all the night noises into one great note that came simultaneously from all quarters of the horizon, infinitely vast, infinitely deep—a steady diapason strain like the undermost bourdon of a great organ as the wind begins to thrill the pipes.

It was the stir of life, the breathing of the Colossus, the push of the nethermost basic force, old as the world, wide as the world, the murmur of the primeval energy, coeval with the centuries, blood brother to that spirit which, in the brooding darkness before creation, moved upon the face of the waters.

And besides this, as Verrill stood there looking out, the night wind brought to him, along with the taint of the sea, the odor of the heaped-up fruit in the city's markets and even the suggestion of the vegetable gardens in the suburbs.

Across his face, like the passing of a long breath, he felt the abrupt sensation of life, indestructible, persistent.

But absorbed in other things, Verrill, unmoved, and only dimly comprehending, closed the window and turned back into the room. At his place stood an unopened bottle and a glass as yet dry. He removed the foil from the neck of the bottle, but after looking at his watch, set it down again without drawing the cork. It lacked some fifteen minutes to midnight.

Once again, as he had already done so many times that evening, Verrill wiped the moisture from his forehead. He shut his teeth against the slow, thick laboring of his heart. He was alone. The sense of isolation, of abandonment, weighed down upon him intolerably as he looked up and down the empty table. Alone, alone; all the rest were gone, and he stood there, in the solitude of that midnight; he, last of all that company whom he had known and loved. Over and over again he muttered:

"All, all are gone, the old familiar faces." Then slowly Verrill began to make the circuit of the table, reading, as if from a roll call, the names written on the cards which lay upon the place plates. "Anderson,...Evans,...Copeland—dear old 'crooked-face' Copeland, his camp companion in those Maine fishing trips of the old days, dead now these ten years.... Stryker—'Buff' Stryker they had called him, dead—he had forgotten how long—drowned in his yacht off the Massachusetts coast; Harris, died of typhoid somewhere in Italy; Dick Herndon, killed in a mine accident in Mexico; Rice, old 'Whitey Rice,' a suicide in a California cattle town; Curtice, carried off by fever in Durban, South Africa." Thus around the whole table he moved, telling the beadroll of death, following in the footsteps of the Monster who never relented, who never tired, who never, never, never forgot.

His own turn would come someday. Verrill, sunken into his chair, put his hands over his eyes. Yes, his own turn would come. There was no escape. That dreadful face would rise again before his eyes. He would bow his back to the scourge of nations, he would roll helpless beneath the wheels of the great car. How to face that prospect with fortitude! How to look into those terrible gray eyes with calm! Oh, the terror of that gorgon face, oh, the horror of those sightless, lightless gray eyes!

But suddenly midnight struck. He heard the strokes come booming upward from the city streets. His vigil was all but over.

Verrill opened the bottle of wine, breaking the seal that had been affixed to the cork on the night of the first meeting of the club. Filling his glass, he rose in his place. His eyes swept the table, and while for the last time the memories came thronging back, his lips formed the words:

"To the Absent Ones: to you, Curtice, Anderson, Brill; to you, Copeland; to you, Stryker; to you, Arnold; to you all, my old comrades, all you old familiar faces who are absent tonight."

He emptied the glass, but immediately filled it again. The last toast was to be drunk, the last of all. Verrill, the glass raised, straightened himself.

But even as he stood there, glass in hand, he shivered slightly. He made note of it for the moment, yet his emotions had so shaken him during all that evening that he could well understand the little shudder that passed over him for a moment.

But he caught himself glancing at the windows. All were shut. The doors of the hall were closed, the flames of the chandeliers were steady. Whence came then this certain sense of coolness that so suddenly had invaded the air? The coolness was not disagreeable, but nonetheless the temperature of the room had been lowered, at least so he could fancy. Yet already he was dismissing the matter from his mind. No doubt the weather had changed suddenly.

In the next second, however, another peculiar circumstance forced itself upon his attention. The stillness of the Banquet Hall, placed as it was at the top of one of the highest buildings in the city, was no matter of comment to Verrill. He was long since familiar with it. But for all that, even through the closed windows, and through the medium of steel and brick and marble that composed the building the indefinite murmur of the city's streets had always made itself felt in the hall. It was faint, yet it was distinct. That bourdon of life to which he had listened that very evening was not wholly to be shut out, yet now, even in this supreme moment of the occasion, it was impossible for Verrill to ignore the fancy that an unusual stillness had all at once widened about him, like the widening of unseen ripples. There was not a sound, and he told himself that stillness such as this was only the portion of the deaf. No faintest tremor of noise rose from the streets. The vast building itself had suddenly grown as soundless as the unplumbed depth of the sea. But Verrill shook himself; all evening fancies such as these had besieged him, even now they were prolonging the ordeal. Once this last toast drunk and he was released from his duty. He raised his glass again, and then in a loud, clear voice he said:

"*Gentlemen, I give you the toast of the evening.*" And as he emptied the glass, a quick, light footstep sounded in the corridor outside the door.

Verrill looked up in great annoyance. The corridor led to but one place, the door of the Banquet Hall, and anyone coming down the corridor at so brisk a pace could have but one intention—that of entering the hall. Verrill frowned at the idea of an intruder. His orders had been of the strictest. That a stranger should thrust himself upon his company at this of all moments was exasperating.

But the footsteps drew nearer, and as Verrill stood frowning at the door at the far end of the hall, it opened.

A gentleman came in, closed the door behind him, and faced about. Verrill scrutinized him with an intent eye.

He was faultlessly dressed, and just by his manner of carrying himself in his evening clothes Verrill knew that here was breeding, distinction. The newcomer was tall, slim. Also he was young; Verrill, though he could not have placed his age with any degree of accuracy, would nonetheless have disposed of the question by setting him down as a young man. But Verrill further observed that the gentleman was very pale, even his lips lacked color. However, as he looked closer, he discovered that this pallor was hardly the result of any present emotion, but was rather constitutional.

There was a moment's silence as the two looked at each other the length of the Hall; then with a peculiarly pleasant smile the stranger came forward drawing off his white glove and extending his hand. He seemed so at home, so perfectly at his ease, and at the same time so much of what Verrill was wont to call a "thoroughbred fellow" that the latter found it impossible to cherish any resentment. He preferred to believe that the stranger had made some readily explained mistake which would be rectified in their first spoken words. Thus it was that he was all the more non-plussed when the stranger took him by the hand with the words: "This is Mr. Manning Verrill, of course. I am very glad to meet you again, sir. Two such as you and I who have once been so intimate should never forget each other."

Verrill had it upon his lips to inform the other that he had something the advantage of him; but at the last moment he was unable to utter the words. The newcomer's pleasure in the meeting was so hearty, so spontaneous, that he could not quite bring himself to jeopardize it—at the outset at least—by a confession of implied unfriendliness; so instead he clumsily assumed the other's manner, and, though deeply perplexed, managed to attain a certain heartiness as he exclaimed: "But you have come very late. I have already dined, and by the way, let me explain why you find me here alone, in a deserted banquet hall with covers laid for so many."

"Indeed, you need not explain," replied the stranger. "I am a member of your club, you know."

A member of the club, this total stranger! Verrill could not hide a frown of renewed perplexity; surely this face was not one of any friend he ever had. "A charter member, you might say," the other continued; "but singularly enough, I have never been able to attend one of the meetings until now. Of us all I think I have been the busiest—and the one most widely traveled. Such must be my excuses."

At the moment an explanation occurred to Verrill. It was within the range of the possible that the newcomer was an old member of the club, some sojourner in a foreign country, whose death had been falsely reported. Possibly Verrill had lost track of him. It was not always easy to "place" at once every one of the thirty. The two sat down, but almost immediately Verrill exclaimed:

"Pardon me, but—that chair. The omen would be so portentous! You have taken the wrong place. You who are a member of the club! You must remember that we reserved that chair—the one you are occupying."

But the stranger smiled calmly.

"I defy augury, and I snap my fingers at the portent. Here is my place and here I choose to remain."

"As you will," answered Verrill, "but it is a singular choice. It is not conducive to appetite."

"My dear Verrill," answered the other, "I shall not dine, if you will permit me to say so. It is very late and my time is limited. I can stay but a short while at best. I have much to do tonight after I leave you—much good I hope, much good. For which," he added rather sadly, "I shall receive no thanks, only abuse, only abuse, my dear Verrill." Verrill was only half listening. He was looking at the other's face, and as he looked he wondered; for the brow was of the kind fitted for crowns, and from beneath glowed the glance of a king. The mouth seemed to have been shaped by the utterance of the commands of empire. The whole face was astonishing, full of power tempered by a great kindliness. Verrill could not keep his gaze from those wonderful, calm gray eyes. Who was this extraordinary man met under such strange circumstances, alone and in the night, in the midst of so many dead memories, and surrounded by that inexplicable stillness, that sudden, profound peace? And what was the subtle magnetism that upon sight drew him so powerfully to the stranger? Kingly he was, but Verrill seemed to feel that he was more than that. He was—could be—a friend, such a friend as in all their circle of dead companions he had never known. In his company he knew he need never be ashamed of weakness, human, natural, ordained weakness, need not be ashamed because of the certainty of being perfectly and thoroughly understood. Thus it was that when the stranger had spoken the words "—only abuse, only abuse, my dear Verrill," Verrill, starting from his muse, answered quickly: "What, abuse, you! in return for good! You astonish me."

"'Abuse' is the mildest treatment I dare expect; it will no doubt be curses. Of all personages, I am the one most cruelly misunderstood. My friends are few, few, oh, so pitiably few."

"Of whom may I be one?" exclaimed Verrill.

"I hope," said the stranger gravely, "we shall be the best of friends. When we met before I am afraid, my appearance was too abrupt and—what shall I say?—unpleasant to win your good will." Verrill, in some embarrassment, framed a lame reply; but the other continued:

"You do not remember, as I can easily understand. My manner at that time was against me. It was a whim, but I chose to be most forbidding on that occasion. I am a very Harlequin in my moods; Harlequin did I say, my dear fellow? I am the Prince of Masqueraders."

"But a prince in all events," murmured Verrill, half to himself.

"Prince and slave," returned the other, "slave to circumstance."

"Are we not all——" began Verrill, but the stranger continued:

"Slave to circumstance, slave to time, slave to natural laws, none so abject as I, in my servility. When the meanest, the lowest, the very weakest calls, I must obey. On the other hand, none so despotic as I, none so absolute. When I summon, the strongest must respond; when I command, the most powerful must obey. My profession, my dear Verrill, is an arduous one."

"Your profession is, I take it," observed Verrill, "that of a physician."

"You may say so," replied the other, "and you may also say an efficient one. But I am always the last to be summoned. I am a last resource; my remedy is a heroic one. But it prevails—inevitably. No pain, my dear Verrill, so sharp that I cannot allay, no anguish so great that I cannot soothe."

"Then perhaps you may prescribe for me," said Verrill. "Of late I have been perturbed. I have lived under a certain strain, certain contingencies threaten, which, no doubt unreasonably, I have come to dread. I am shaken, nervous, fearful. My own doctor has been unable to help me. Perhaps you——"

The stranger had already opened the bottle of wine which stood by his plate, and filled the silver cup. He handed it to Verrill.

"Drink," he said.

Verrill hesitated.

"But this wine," he protested. "This cup—pardon me, it was reserved——"

"Drink," repeated the stranger. "Trust me."

He took Verrill's glass in which he had drunk the toasts and which yet contained a little wine. He pressed the silver cup into Verrill's hands.

"Drink," he urged for the third time.

Verrill took the cup, and the stranger raised his glass.

"To our better acquaintance," he said.

But Verrill, at length at the end of all conjecture, cried out, the cup still in his hand:

"Your toast is most appropriate, sir. A better acquaintance with you, I assure you, would be most pleasing to me. But I must ask your pardon for my stupidity. Where have we met before? Who are you, and what is your name?"

The stranger did not immediately reply, but fixed his grave gray eyes upon Verrill's. For a moment he held his gaze in his own. Then as the seconds slipped by, the first indefinite sense of suspicion flashed across Verrill's mind, flashed and faded, returned once more, faded again, and left him wondering. Then as the stranger said:

"Do you remember?—it was long ago. Do you remember the sight of naked spars rocking against a gray torn sky, a ship wrenching and creaking, wrestling with the wind, a world of pale green surges, the gale singing through the cordage, and then as the sea swept the decks? Ah, you *do* remember."

For Verrill had started suddenly, and with the movement, full recognition, complete, unequivocal, gleamed suddenly in his eyes. There was a long silence while he returned the gaze of the other, now no longer a stranger. At length Verrill spoke, drawing a long breath:

"Ah . . . it is you . . . at last."

"Well!"

Verrill smiled.

"It *is* well, I had imagined it would be so different—when you did come. But as it is," he extended his hand, "I am very glad to meet you."

"Did I not tell you," said the other, "that of all the world, I am the most cruelly misunderstood?"

"But you confessed to the masquerade."

"Oh, blind, blind, not to see behind the foolish mask. Come, we have not yet drunk."

He placed the cup in Verrill's hands, and once again raised the glass.

"To our better acquaintance," he said.

"To our better acquaintance," echoed Verrill. He drained the cup. "The lees were bitter," he observed.

"But the effect?"

"Yes, it is calming—already, exquisitely so. It is not—as I have imagined for so long, deadening; on the contrary, it is invigorating, revivifying. I feel born again."

The other rose. "Then there is no need," he said, "to stay here any longer. Come, shall we be going?"

"Yes, yes, I am ready," answered Verrill. "Look," he exclaimed, pointing to the windows. "Look—it is morning."

Low in the east, the dawn was rising over the city. A new day was coming; the stars were paling, the night was over.

"That is true," said Verrill's new friend. "Another day is coming. It is time we went out to meet it."

They rose and passed down the length of the Banquet Hall. He who had called himself the great Physician, the Servant of the Humble, the Master of Kings, the Prince of Masqueraders, held open the door for Verrill to pass. But when the man had gone out, the Prince paused a moment, and looked back upon the deserted Banquet Hall, lit partly by the steady electrics, partly by the pale light of morning, that now began with ever-increasing radiance to stream through the eastern windows. Then he stretched forth his hand and laid his touch upon a button in the wall. Instantly the lights sank, vanished; for a moment the hall seemed dark.

He went out quietly, shutting the door behind him.

And the Banquet Hall remained deserted, lonely, empty, yet it was neither dark nor lifeless. Stronger and stronger grew the flood of light that burned roseate toward the zenith as the sun came up. It penetrated to every corner of the room, and the drops of wine left in the bottom of the glasses flashed like jewels in the radiance. From without, from the city's streets, came the murmur of increasing activity. Through the night it had droned on, like the low-pitched diapason of some vast organ, but now as the sun rose, it swelled in volume. Louder it grew and ever louder. Its sound waves beat upon the windows of the hall. They invaded the hall itself.

It was the symphony of energy, the vast orchestration of force, the paean of an indestructible life, coeval with the centuries, renascent, ordained, eternal.

A MEMORANDUM OF SUDDEN DEATH

The manuscript of the account that follows belongs to a harness maker in Albuquerque, Juan Tejada by name, and he is welcome to whatever of advertisement this notice may bring him. He is a good fellow, and his patented martingale for stage horses may be recommended. I understand he got the manuscript from a man named Bass, or possibly Bass left it with him for safekeeping. I know that Tejada has some things of Bass's now—things that Bass left with him last November: a mess kit, a lantern and a broken theodolite—a whole saddle box full of contraptions. I forgot to ask Tejada how Bass got the manuscript, and I wish I had done so now, for the finding of it might be a story itself. The probabilities are that Bass simply picked it up page by page off the desert, blown about the spot where the fight occurred and at some little distance from the bodies. Bass, I am told, is a bone gatherer by profession, and one can easily understand how he would come across the scene of the encounter in one of his tours into western Arizona. My interest in the affair is impersonal, but nonetheless keen. Though I did not know young Karslake, I knew his stuff— as everybody still does, when you come to that. For the matter of that, the mere mention of his pen name, "Anson Qualtraugh," recalls at once to thousands of the readers of a certain world-famous monthly magazine of New York articles and stories he wrote for it while he was alive; as, for instance, his admirable descriptive work called "Traces of the Aztecs on the Mogolon Mesa," in the October number of 1890. Also, in the January issue of 1892 there are two specimens of his work, one signed Anson Qualtraugh and the other Justin Blisset. Why he should have used the Blisset signature I do not know. It occurs only this once in all his writings. In this case it is signed to a very indifferent New Year's story. The Qualtraugh "stuff" of the same number is, so the editor writes to me, a much shortened transcript of a monograph on "Primitive Methods of Moki Irrigation," which are now in the archives of the Smithsonian. The admirable novel, *The Peculiar Treasure of Kings*, is of course well known. Karslake wrote it in 1888-89, and the controversy that arose about the incident of the third chapter is still—sporadically and intermittently—continued.

The manuscript that follows now appears, of course, for the first time in print, and I acknowledge herewith my obligations to Karslake's father, Mr. Patterson Karslake, for permission to publish.

I have set the account down word for word, with all the hiatuses and breaks that by nature of the extraordinary circumstances under which it was written were bound to appear in it. I have allowed it to end precisely as Karslake was forced to end it, in the middle of a sentence. God knows the real end is plain enough and was not far off when the poor fellow began the last phrase that never was to be finished.

The value of the thing is self-apparent. Besides the narrative of incidents it is a simple setting forth of a young man's emotions in the very face of violent death. You will remember the distinguished victim of the guillotine, a lady who on the scaffold begged that she might be permitted to write out the great thoughts that began to throng her mind. She was not allowed to do so, and the record is lost. Here is a case where the record is preserved. But Karslake, being a young man not very much given to introspection, his work is more a picture of things seen than a transcription of things thought. However, one may read between the lines; the very breaks are eloquent, while the break at the end speaks with a significance that no words could attain.

The manuscript in itself is interesting. It is written partly in pencil, partly in ink (no doubt from a fountain pen), on sheets of manila paper torn from some sort of long and narrow account book. In two or three places there are smudges where the powder-blackened finger and thumb held the sheets momentarily. I would give much to own it, but Tejada will not give it up without Bass's permission, and Bass has gone to the Klondike.

As to Karslake himself. He was born in Raleigh, in North Carolina, in 1868, studied law at the State University, and went to the Bahamas in 1885 with the members of a government coast survey commission. Gave up the practice of law and "went in" for fiction and the study of the ethnology of North America about 1887. He was unmarried.

The reasons for his enlisting have long been misunderstood. It was known that at the time of his death he was a member of B Troop of the Sixth Regiment of United States Cavalry, and it was assumed that because of this fact Karslake was in financial difficulties and not upon good terms with his family. All this, of course, is untrue, and I have every reason to believe that Karslake at this time was planning a novel of military life in the Southwest, and, wishing to get in closer touch with the milieu of the story, actually enlisted in order to be able to write authoritatively. He saw no active service until the time when his narrative begins. The year of his death is uncertain. It was in the spring probably of 1896, in the twenty-eighth year of his age.

There is no doubt he would have become in time a great writer. A young man of twenty-eight who had so lively a sense of the value of accurate observation, and so eager a desire to produce that in the very face of death he could faithfully set down a description of his surroundings, actually laying down the rifle to pick up the pen, certainly was possessed of extraordinary faculties.

"They came in sight early this morning just after we had had breakfast and had broken camp. The four of us—'Bunt,' 'Idaho,' Estorijo and myself—were jogging on to the southward and had just come up out of the dry bed of some water hole—the alkali was white as snow in the crevices—when Idaho pointed them out to us, three to the rear, two on one side, one on the other and— very far away—two ahead. Five minutes before, the desert was as empty as the flat of my hand. They seemed literally to have *grown* out of the sagebrush. We took them in through my field glasses and Bunt made sure they were an outlying band of Hunt-in-the-Morning's bucks. I had thought, and so had all of us, that the rest of the boys had rounded up the whole of the old man's hostiles long since. We are at a loss to account for these fellows here. They seem to be well mounted.

"We held a council of war from the saddle without halting, but there seemed very little to be done—but to go right along and wait for developments. At about eleven we found water—just a pocket in the bed of a dried stream—and stopped to water the ponies. I am writing this during the halt.

"We have one hundred and sixteen rifle cartridges. Yesterday was Friday, and all day, as the newspapers say, 'the situation remained unchanged.' We expected surely that the night would see some rather radical change, but nothing happened, though we stood watch and watch till morning. Of yesterday's eight only six are in sight and we bring up reserves. We now have two to the front, one on each side, and two to the rear, all far out of rifle range.

[*The following paragraph is in an unsteady script and would appear to have been written in the saddle. The same peculiarity occurs from time to time in the narrative, and occasionally the writing is so broken as to be illegible.*]

"On again after breakfast. It is about eight-fifteen. The other two have come back—without 'reserves,' thank God. Very possibly they did not go away at all, but were hidden by a dip in the ground. I cannot see that any of them are nearer. I have watched one to the left of us steadily for more than half an hour and I am sure that he has not shortened the distance between himself and us. What their plans are Hell only knows, but this silent, persistent escorting tells on the nerves. I do not think I am afraid—as yet. It does not seem possible but that we will ride into La Paz at the end of the fortnight exactly as we had planned, meet Greenock according to arrangements and take the stage on to the railroad. Then next month I shall be in San Antonio and report at headquarters. Of course, all this is to be, of course; and this business of today will make a good story to tell. It's an experience—good 'material.' Very naturally I cannot now see how I am going to get out of this" [*the word "alive" has here been erased*], "but of course I *will*. Why 'of course'? I don't know. Maybe I am trying to deceive myself. Frankly, it looks like a situation insoluble; but the solution will surely come right enough in good time.

"Eleven o'clock.—No change.

"Two-thirty P. M.—We are halted to tighten girths and to take a single swallow of the canteens. One of them rode in a wide circle from the rear to the flank, about ten minutes ago, conferred a moment with his fellow, then fell back to his old position. He wears some sort of red cloth or blanket. We reach no more water till day after tomorrow. But we have sufficient. Estorijo has been telling funny stories en route.

"Four o'clock P. M.—They have closed up perceptibly, and we have been debating about trying one of them with Idaho's Winchester. No use; better save the ammunition. It looks. . . ." [*the next words are undecipherable, but from the context they would appear to be "as if they would attack tonight"*] ". . . we have come to know certain of them now by nicknames. We speak of the Red One, or the Little One, or the One with the Feather, and Idaho has named a short thickset fellow on our right 'Little Willie.' By God, I wish something would turn up—relief or fight. I don't care which. How Estorijo can cackle on, reeling off his senseless, pointless funny stories, is beyond me. Bunt is almost as bad. They understand the fix we are in, I *know*, but how they can take it so easily is the staggering surprise. I feel that I am as courageous as either of them, but levity seems horribly inappropriate. I could kill Estorijo joyfully.

"Sunday morning.—Still no developments. We were so sure of something turning up last night that none of us pretended to sleep. But nothing stirred. There is no sneaking out of the circle at night. The moon is full. A jackrabbit could not have slipped by them unseen last night.

"Nine o'clock (in the saddle).—We had coffee and bacon as usual at sunrise; then on again to the southeast just as before. For half an hour after starting the Red One and two others were well within rifle shot, nearer than ever before. They had worked in from the flank. But before Idaho could get a chance at them they dipped into a shallow arroyo, and when they came out on the other side were too far away to think of shooting.

"Ten o'clock.—All at once we find there are nine instead of eight; where and when this last one joined the band we cannot tell. He wears a sombrero and army trousers, but the upper part of his body is bare. Idaho calls him 'Half-and-half.' He is riding a—— They're coming.

"Later.—For a moment we thought it was the long-expected rush. The Red One—he had been in the front—wheeled quick as a flash and came straight for us, and the others followed suit.

Great Heavens, how they rode! We could hear them yelling on every side of us. We jumped off our ponies and stood behind them, the rifles across the saddles. But at four hundred yards they all pivoted about and cantered off again leisurely. Now they followed us as before—three in the front, two in the rear and two on either side. I do not think I am going to be frightened when the rush does come. I watched myself just now. I was excited, and I remember Bunt saying to me, 'Keep your shirt on, m'son'; but I was not afraid of being killed. Thank God for that! It is something I've long wished to find out, and now that I know it I am proud of it. Neither side fired a shot. I was not afraid. It's glorious. Estorijo is all right.

"Sunday afternoon, one-thirty.—No change. It is unspeakably hot.

"Three-fifteen.—The One with the Feather is walking, leading his pony. It seems to be lame." [*With this entry Karslake ended page five, and the next page of the manuscript is numbered seven. It is very probable, however, that he made a mistake in the numerical sequence of his pages, for the narrative is continuous, and, at this point at least, unbroken. There does not seem to be any sixth page.*]

"Four o'clock.—Is it possible that we are to pass another night of suspense? They certainly show no signs of bringing on the crisis, and they surely would not attempt anything so late in the afternoon as this. It is a relief to feel that we have nothing to fear till morning, but the tension of watching all night long is fearful.

"Later.—Idaho has just killed the Little One.

"Later.—Still firing.

"Later.—Still at it.

"Later, about five.—A bullet struck within three feet of me.

"Five-ten.—Still firing.

"Seven-thirty P. M., in camp.—It happened so quickly that it was all over before I realized. We had our first interchange of shots with them late this afternoon. The Little One was riding from the front to the flank. Evidently he did not think he was in range—nor did any of us. All at once Idaho tossed up his rifle and let go without aiming—or so it seemed to me. The stock was not at his shoulder before the report came. About six seconds after the smoke had cleared away we could see the Little One begin to lean backward in the saddle, and Idaho said grimly, 'I guess I got *you.*' The Little One leaned farther and farther till suddenly his head dropped back between his shoulder blades. He held to his pony's mane with both hands for a long time and then all at once went off feet first. His legs bent under him like putty as his feet touched the ground. The pony bolted.

"Just as soon as Idaho fired the others closed right up and began riding around us at top speed, firing as they went. Their aim was bad as a rule, but one bullet came very close to me. At about half-past five they drew off out of range again and we made camp right where we stood. Estorijo and I are both sure that Idaho hit the Red One, but Idaho himself is doubtful, and Bunt did not see the shot. I could swear that the Red One all but went off his pony. However, he seems active enough now.

"Monday morning.—Still another night without attack. I have not slept since Friday evening. The strain is terrific. At daybreak this morning, when one of our ponies snorted suddenly, I cried out at the top of my voice. I could no more have repressed it than I could have stopped my blood flowing; and for half an hour afterward I could feel my flesh crisping and pringling, and there was a sickening weakness at the pit of my stomach. At breakfast I had to force down my coffee. They are still in place, but now there are two on each side, two in the front, two in the rear. The killing of the Little One seems to have heartened us all wonderfully. I am sure we will get out—somehow. But oh! the suspense of it.

"Monday morning, nine-thirty.—Under way for over two hours. There is no new development. But Idaho has just said that they seem to be edging in. We hope to reach water today. Our supply is low, and the ponies are beginning to hang their heads. It promises to be a blazing hot day. There is alkali all to the west of us, and we just commence to see the rise of ground miles to the southward that Idaho says is the San Jacinto Mountains. Plenty of water there. The desert hereabout is vast and lonesome beyond words; leagues of sparse sagebrush, leagues of leper-white alkali, leagues of baking gray sand; empty, heat-ridden, the abomination of desolation; and always—in whichever direction I turn my eyes—always, in the midst of this pale-yellow blur, a single figure in the distance, blanketed, watchful, solitary, standing out sharp and distinct against the background of sage and sand.

"Monday, about eleven o'clock.—No change. The heat is appalling. There is just a——

"Later.—I was on the point of saying that there was just a mouthful of water left for each of us in our canteens when Estorijo and Idaho both at the same time cried out that they were moving in. It is true. They are within rifle range, but do not fire. We, as well, have decided to reserve our fire until something more positive happens.

"Noon.—The first shot—for today—from the Red One. We are halted. The shot struck low and to the left. We could see the sand spout up in a cloud just as though a bubble had burst on the surface of the ground.

"They have separated from each other, and the whole eight of them are now in a circle around us. Idaho believes the Red One fired as a signal. Estorijo is getting ready to take a shot at the One with the Feather. We have the ponies in a circle around us. It looks as if now at last this was the beginning of the real business.

"Later, twelve-thirty-five.—Estorijo missed. Idaho will try with the Winchester as soon as the One with the Feather halts. He is galloping toward the Red One.

"All at once, about two o'clock, the fighting began. This is the first letup. It is now—God knows what time. They closed up suddenly and began galloping about us in a circle, firing all the time. They rode like madmen. I would not have believed that Indian ponies could run so quickly. What with their yelling and the incessant crack of their rifles and the thud of their ponies' feet our horses at first became very restless, and at last Idaho's mustang bolted clean away. We all stood to it as hard as we could. For about the first fifteen minutes it was hot work. The Spotted One is hit. We are certain of that much, though we do not know whose gun did the work. My poor old horse is bleeding dreadfully from the mouth. He has two bullets in the stomach, and I do not believe he can stand much longer. They have let up for the last few moments, but are still riding around us, their guns at 'ready.' Every now and then one of us fires, but the heat shimmer has come up over the ground since noon and the range is extraordinarily deceiving.

"Three-ten.—Estorijo's horse is down, shot clean through the head. Mine has gone long since. We have made a rampart of the bodies.

"Three-twenty.—They are at it again, tearing around us incredibly fast, every now and then narrowing the circle. The bul-

lets are striking everywhere now. I have no rifle, do what I can with my revolver, and try to watch what is going on in front of me and warn the others when they press in too close on my side."
[*Karslake nowhere accounts for the absence of his carbine. That a U. S. trooper should be without his gun while traversing a hostile country is a fact difficult to account for.*]

"Three-thirty.—They have winged me—through the shoulder. Not bad, but it is bothersome. I sit up to fire, and Bunt gives me his knee on which to rest my right arm. When it hangs it is painful.

"Quarter to four.—It is horrible. Bunt is dying. He cannot speak, the ball having gone through the lower part of his face, but back, near the neck. It happened through his trying to catch his horse. The animal was struck in the breast and tried to bolt. He reared up, backing away, and as we had to keep him close to us to serve as a bulwark Bunt followed him out from the little circle that we formed, his gun in one hand, his other gripping the bridle. I suppose every one of the eight fired at him simultaneously, and down he went. The pony dragged him a little ways still clutching the bridle, then fell itself, its whole weight rolling on Bunt's chest. We have managed to get him in and secure his rifle, but he will not live. None of us knows him very well. He only joined us about a week ago, but we all liked him from the start. He never spoke of himself, so we cannot tell much about him. Idaho says he has a wife in Torreon, but that he has not lived with her for two years; they did not get along well together, it seems. This is the first violent death I have ever seen, and it astonishes me to note how *unimportant* it seems. How little anybody cares— after all. If I had been told of his death—the details of it, in a story or in the form of fiction—it is easily conceivable that it would have impressed me more with its importance than the actual scene has done. Possibly my mental vision is scaled to a larger field since Friday, and as the greater issues loom up one man more or less seems to be but a unit—more or less—in an eternal series. When he was hit he swung back against the horse, still holding by the rein. His feet slid from under him, and he cried out, 'My *God!*' just once. We divided his cartridges between us and Idaho passed me his carbine. The barrel was scorching hot.

"They have drawn off a little and for fifteen minutes, though they still circle us slowly, there has been no firing. Forty cartridges left. Bunt's body (I think he is dead now) lies just back of me, and already the gnats—I can't speak of it."

[*Karslake evidently made the next few entries at successive intervals of time, but neglected in his excitement to note the exact hour as above. We may gather that "They" made another attack and then repeated the assault so quickly that he had no chance to record it properly. I transcribe the entries in exactly the disjointed manner in which they occur in the original. The reference to the "fire" is unexplainable.*]

"I shall do my best to set down exactly what happened and what I do and think, and what I see.

"The heat shimmer spoiled my aim, but I am quite sure that either

"This last rush was the nearest. I had started to say that though the heat shimmer was bad, either Estorijo or myself wounded one of their ponies. We saw him stumble.

"Another rush——

"Our ammunition

"Only a few cartridges left.

"The Red One like a whirlwind only fifty yards away

"We fire separately now as they sneak up under cover of our smoke.

"We put the fire out. Estorijo——" [*It is possible that Karslake had begun here to chronicle the death of the Mexican.*]

"I have killed the Spotted One. Just as he wheeled his horse I saw him in a line with the rifle sights and let him have it squarely. It took him straight in the breast. I could *feel* that shot strike. He went down like a sack of lead weights. By God, it was superb!

"Later.—They have drawn off out of range again, and we are allowed a breathing spell. Our ponies are either dead or dying, and we have dragged them around us to form a barricade. We lie on the ground behind the bodies and fire over them. There are twenty-seven cartridges left.

"It is now mid-afternoon. Our plan is to stand them off if we can till night and then to try an escape between them. But to what purpose? They would trail us so soon as it was light.

"We think now that they followed us without attacking for so long because they were waiting till the lay of the land suited them. They wanted—no doubt—an absolutely flat piece of country, with no depressions, no hills or streambeds in which we could hide, but which should be high upon the edges, like an amphitheater. They would get us in the center and occupy the rim themselves. Roughly, this is the bit of desert which witnesses our 'last stand.' On three sides the ground swells a very little—the rise is not four feet. On the third side it is open, and so flat that even lying on the ground as we do we can see (leagues away) the San Jacinto hills—'from whence cometh no help.' It is all sand and sage, forever and forever. Even the sage is sparse—a bad place even for a coyote. The whole is flagellated with an intolerable heat and—now that the shooting is relaxed—oppressed with a benumbing, sodden silence—the silence of a primordial world. Such a silence as must have brooded over the Face of the Waters on the Eve of Creation—desolate, desolate, as though a colossal, invisible pillar—a pillar of the Infinitely Still, the pillar of Nirvana—rose forever into the empty blue, human life an atom of microscopic dust crushed under its basis, and at the summit God Himself. And I find time to ask myself why, at this of all moments of my tiny life span, I am able to write as I do, registering impressions, keeping a finger upon the pulse of the spirit. But oh! if I had time now—time to write down the great thoughts that do throng the brain. They are there, I feel them, know them. No doubt the supreme exaltation of approaching death is the stimulus that one never experiences in the humdrum business of the day-to-day existence. Such mighty thoughts! Unintelligible, but if I had time I could spell them out, *and how I could write then!* I feel that the whole secret of Life is within my reach; I can almost grasp it; I seem to feel that in just another instant I can see it all plainly, as the archangels see it all the time, as the great minds of the world, the great philosophers, have seen it once or twice, vaguely—a glimpse here and there, after years of patient study. Seeing thus I should be the equal of the gods. But it is not meant to be. There is a sacrilege in it. I almost seem to understand why it is kept from us. But the very reason of this withholding is in itself a part of the secret. If I could only, only set it down!—for whose eyes? Those of a wandering hawk? God knows. But never mind. I should have spoken—once; should have said the great Word for which the World since the evening and the morning of the First Day has listened. God knows. God knows. What a whirl is this? Monstrous incongruity. Philosophy and fighting troopers. The Infinite and dead horses. There's humor for you. The Sublime takes off its hat to the Ridiculous. Send a cartridge clashing into the breech and speculate about the Absolute. Keep one eye on your sights and the other on Cosmos. Blow the reek of burned powder from before you so you may look over the edge of the abyss of the Great Primal Cause. Duck to the whistle of a bullet and commune with Schopenhauer. Perhaps I am a little mad. Perhaps I am supremely intelligent. But in either case I am not understandable to myself. How, then, be understandable to others? If these sheets of paper, this incoherence, is ever read, the others will understand it about as much as the investigating hawk. But nonetheless be it of record that I, Karslake, *saw*. It reads like Revelations: 'I, John, saw.' It is just that. There is something apocalyptic in it all. I have seen a vision, but cannot—there is the pitch of anguish in the impotence—bear record. If time were allowed to order and arrange the words of description, this exaltation of spirit, in that very space of time, would relax, and the describer lapse back to the level of the average again before he could set down the things he saw, the things he thought. The machinery of the mind that could coin the great Word is automatic, and the very force that brings the die near the blank metal supplies the motor power of the reaction before the impression is made.... I stopped for an instant, looking up from the page, and at once the great vague panorama faded. I lost it all. Cosmos has dwindled again to an amphitheater of sage and sand, a vista of distant purple hills, the shimmer of scorching alkali, and in the middle distance there, those figures, blanketed, beaded, feathered, rifle in hand.

"But for a moment I stood on Patmos.

"The Ridiculous jostles the elbow of the Sublime and shoulders it from place as Idaho announces that he has found two more cartridges in Estorijo's pockets.

"They rushed again. Eight more cartridges gone. Twenty-one left. They rush in this manner—at first the circle, rapid beyond expression, one figure succeeding the other so swiftly that the dizzied vision loses count and instead of seven of them there appear to be seventy. Then suddenly, on some indistinguishable signal, they contract this circle, and through the jets of powder smoke Idaho and I see them whirling past our rifle sights not one hundred yards away. Then their fire suddenly slackens, the smoke drifts by, and we see them in the distance again, moving about us at a slow canter. Then the blessed breathing spell, while we peer out to know if we have killed or not, and count our cartridges. We have laid the twenty-one loaded shells that remain in a row between us, and after our first glance outward to see if any of them are down, our next is inward at that ever-shrinking line of brass and lead. We do not talk much. This is the end. We know it now. All of a sudden the conviction that I am to die here has hardened within me. It is, all at once, absurd that I should ever have supposed that I was to reach La Paz, take the eastbound train and report at San Antonio. It seems to me that I *knew*, weeks ago, that our trip was to end thus. I knew it—somehow—in Sonora, while we were waiting orders, and I tell myself that if I had only stopped to really think of it I could have foreseen today's bloody business.

"Later.—The Red One got off his horse and bound up the creature's leg. One of us hit him, evidently. A little higher, it would have reached the heart. Our aim is ridiculously bad—the heat shimmer——

"Later.—Idaho is wounded. This last time, for a moment, I was sure the end had come. They were within revolver range and we could feel the vibration of the ground under their ponies' hoofs. But suddenly they drew off. I have looked at my watch; it is four o'clock.

"Four o'clock.—Idaho's wound is bad—a long, raking furrow in the right forearm. I bind it up for him, but he is losing a great deal of blood and is very weak.

"They seem to know that we are only two by now, for with each rush they grow bolder. The slackening of our fire must tell them how scant is our ammunition.

"Later.—This last was magnificent. The Red One and one other with lines of blue paint across his cheek galloped right at us. Idaho had been lying with his head and shoulders propped against the neck of his dead pony. His eyes were shut, and I thought he had fainted. But as he heard them coming he struggled up, first to his knees and then to his feet—to his full height—dragging his revolver from his hip with his left hand. The whole right arm swung useless. He was so weak that he could only lift the revolver halfway—could not get the muzzle up. But though it sagged and dropped in his grip, he *would* die fighting. When he fired the bullet threw up the sand not a yard from his feet, and then he fell on his face across the body of the horse. During the charge I fired as fast as I could, but evidently to no purpose. They must have thought that Idaho was dead, for as soon as they saw him getting to his feet they sheered their horses off and went by on either side of us. I have made Idaho comfortable. He is unconscious; have used the last of the water to give him a drink. He does not seem——

"They continue to circle us. Their fire is incessant, but very wild. So long as I keep my head down I am comparatively safe.

"Later.—I think Idaho is dying. It seems he was hit a second time when he stood up to fire. Estorijo is still breathing; I thought him dead long since.

"Four-ten.—Idaho gone. Twelve cartridges left. Am all alone now.

"Four-twenty-five.—I am very weak." [*Karslake was evidently wounded sometime between ten and twenty-five minutes after four. His notes make no mention of the fact.*] "Eight cartridges remain. I leave my library to my brother, Walter Patterson Karslake; all my personal effects to my parents, except the picture of myself taken in Baltimore in 1897, which I direct to be" [*the next lines are undecipherable*] "...at Washington, D. C., as soon as possible. I appoint as my literary

"Four-forty-five.—Seven cartridges. Very weak and unable to move lower part of my body. Am in no pain. They rode in very close. The Red One is—— An intolerable thirst——

"I appoint as my literary executor my brother, Patterson Karslake. The notes on 'Coronado in New Mexico' should be revised.

"My death occurred in western Arizona April 15th, at the hands of a roving band of Hunt-in-the-Morning's bucks. They have——

"Five o'clock.—The last cartridge gone.

"Estorijo still breathing. I cover his face with my hat. Their fire is incessant. Am much weaker. Convey news of death to Patterson Karslake, care of Corn Exchange Bank, New York City.

"Five-fifteen—about.—They have ceased firing, and draw together in a bunch. I have four cartridges left" [*see conflicting note dated five o'clock*], "but am extremely weak. Idaho was the best friend I had in all the Southwest. I wish it to be known that he was a generous, openhearted fellow, a kindly man, clean of speech, and absolutely unselfish. He may be known as follows: Sandy beard, long sandy hair, scar on forehead, about six feet one inch in height. His real name is James Monroe Herndon; his profession that of government scout. Notify Mrs. Herndon, Trinidad, New Mexico.

"The writer is Arthur Staples Karslake, dark hair, height five feet eleven, body will be found near that of Herndon.

"Luis Estorijo, Mexican——

"Later.—Two more cartridges.

"Five-thirty.—Estorijo dead.

"It is half-past five in the afternoon of April fifteenth. They followed us from the eleventh—Friday—till today. It will

[*The MS. ends here.*]

THE PASSING OF COCKEYE BLACKLOCK

"Well m'son," observed Bunt about half an hour after supper, "if your provender has shook down comfortable by now, we might as well jar loose and be moving along out yonder."

We left the fire and moved toward the hobbled ponies, Bunt complaining of the quality of the outfit's meals. "Down in the Panamint country," he growled, "we had a Chink that was a sure frying-pan expert; but *this* Dago—my word! That ain't victuals, that supper. That's just a' ingenious device for removing superfluous appetite. Next time I assimilate nutriment in this camp I'm sure going to take chloroform beforehand. Careful to draw your cinch tight on that pinto bronc' of yours. She always swells up same as a horned toad soon as you begin to saddle up."

We rode from the circle of the camp fire's light and out upon the desert. It was Bunt's turn to ride the herd that night, and I had volunteered to bear him company.

Bunt was one of a fast-disappearing type. He knew his West as the cockney knows his Piccadilly. He had mined with and for Ralston, had soldiered with Crook, had turned cards in a faro game at Laredo, and had known the Apache Kid. He had fifteen separate and different times driven the herds from Texas to Dodge City, in the good old, rare old, wild old days when Dodge was the headquarters for the cattle trade, and as near to heaven as the cowboy cared to get. He had seen the end of gold and the end of the buffalo, the beginning of cattle, the beginning of wheat, and the spreading of the barbed-wire fence, that, in the end, will take from him his occupation and his revolver, his chaparejos and his usefulness, his lariat and his reason for being. He had seen the rise of a new period, the successive stages of which, singularly enough, tally exactly with the progress of our own world-civilization: first the nomad and hunter, then the herder, next and last the husbandman. He had passed the mid-mark of his life. His mustache was gray. He had four friends—his horse, his pistol, a teamster in the Indian Territory Panhandle named Skinny, and me.

The herd—I suppose all told there were some two thousand head—we found not far from the water hole. We relieved the other watch and took up our night's vigil. It was about nine o'clock. The night was fine, calm. There was no cloud. Toward the middle watches one could expect a moon. But the stars, the stars! In Idaho, on those lonely reaches of desert and range, where the shadow of the sun by day and the courses of the constellations by night are the only things that move, these stars are a different matter from those bleared pinpoints of the city after dark, seen through dust and smoke and the glare of electrics and the hot haze of fire-signs. On such a night as that when I rode the herd with Bunt *anything* might have happened; one could have believed in fairies then, and in the buffalo-ghost, and in all the weirds of the craziest Apache "Messiah" that ever made medicine.

One remembered astronomy and the "measureless distances" and the showy problems, including the rapid moving of a ray of light and the long years of its travel between star and star, and smiled incredulously. Why, the stars were just above our heads, were not much higher than the flat-topped hills that barred the horizons. Venus was a yellow lamp hung in a tree; Mars a red lantern in a clock tower.

One listened instinctively for the tramp of the constellations. Orion, Cassiopeia and Ursa Major marched to and fro on the vault like cohorts of legionaries, seemingly within call of our voices, and all without a sound.

But beneath these quiet heavens the earth disengaged multitudinous sounds—small sounds, minimized as it were by the muffling of the night. Now it was the yap of a coyote leagues away; now the snapping of a twig in the sagebrush; now the mysterious, indefinable stir of the heat-ridden land cooling under the night. But more often it was the confused murmur of the herd itself— the click of a horn, the friction of heavy bodies, the stamp of a hoof, with now and then the low, complaining note of a cow with a calf, or the subdued noise of a steer as it lay down, first lurching to the knees, then rolling clumsily upon the haunch, with a long, stertorous breath of satisfaction.

Slowly at Indian trot we encircle the herd. Earlier in the evening a prairie wolf had pulled down a calf, and the beasts were still restless.

Little eddies of nervousness at long intervals developed here and there in the mass—eddies that not impossibly might widen at anytime with perilous quickness to the maelstrom of a stampede. So as he rode Bunt sang to these great brutes, literally to put them to sleep—sang an old grandmother's song, with all the quaint modulations of sixty, seventy, a hundred years ago:

> "With her ogling winks
> And bobbling blinks,
> Her quizzing glass,
> Her one eye idle,
> Oh, she loved a bold dragoon,
> With his broadsword, saddle, bridle.
> *Whack*, fol-de-rol!"

I remember that song. My grandmother—so they tell me—used to sing it in Carolina, in the thirties, accompanying herself on a harp, if you please:

> "Oh, she loved a bold dragoon,
> With his broadsword, saddle, bridle."

It was in Charleston, I remembered, and the slave ships used to discharge there in those days. My grandmother had sung it then to her beaux; officers they were; no wonder she chose it—"Oh, she loved a bold dragoon"—and now I heard it sung on an Idaho cattle range to quiet two thousand restless steers.

Our talk at first, after the cattle had quieted down, ran upon all manner of subjects. It is astonishing to note what strange things men will talk about at night and in a solitude. That night we covered religion, of course, astronomy, love affairs, horses, travel, history, poker, photography, basket making, and the

Darwinian theory. But at last inevitably we came back to cattle and the pleasures and dangers of riding the herd.

"I rode herd once in Nevada," remarked Bunt, "and I was caught into a blizzard, and I was sure freezing to death. Got to where I couldn't keep my eyes open, I was that sleepy. Tell you what I did. Had some eating tobacco along, and I'd chew it a spell, then rub the juice into my eyes. Kept it up all night. Blame near blinded me, but I come through. Me and another man named Blacklock—Cockeye Blacklock we called him, by reason of his having one eye that was some out of line. Cockeye sure ought to have got it that night, for he went bad afterward, and did a heap of killing before he *did* get it. He was a bad man for sure, and the way he died is a story in itself."

There was a long pause. The ponies jogged on. Rounding on the herd, we turned southward.

"He did 'get it' finally, you say," I prompted.

"He certainly did," said Bunt, "and the story of it is what a man with a' imaginary mind like you ought to make into one of your friction tales."

"Is it about a treasure?" I asked with apprehension. For ever since I once made a tale (of friction) out of one of Bunt's stories of real life, he has been ambitious for me to write another, and is forever suggesting motifs which invariably—I say invariably—imply the discovery of great treasures. With him, fictitious literature must always turn upon the discovery of hidden wealth.

"No," said he, "it ain't about no treasure, but just about the origin, hist'ry and development—and subsequent decease—of as mean a Greaser as ever stole stock, which his name was Cockeye Blacklock.

"You see, this same Blacklock went bad about two summers after our meet-up with the blizzard. He worked down Yuma way and over into New Mexico, where he picks up with a sure-thing gambler, and the two begin to devastate the population. They do say when he and his running mate got good and through with that part of the Land of the Brave, men used to go round trading guns for commissary, and clothes for ponies, and cigars for whisky and such. There just wasn't any money left *anywhere*. Those sharps had drawed the landscape clean. Someone found a dollar in a floor crack in a saloon, and the barkeep' gave him a gallon of forty rod for it, and used to keep it in a box for exhibition, and the crowd would get around it and paw it over and say: 'My! my! Whatever in the world is this extremely cu-roos coin?'

"Then Blacklock cuts loose from his running mate, and plays a lone hand through Arizona and Nevada, up as far as Reno again, and there he stacks up against a kid—a little tenderfoot kid so new he ain't cracked the green paint off him—and *skins* him. And the kid, being foolish and impulsive-like, pulls out a peashooter. It was a *twenty-two*," said Bunt, solemnly. "Yes, the kid was just that pore, pathetic kind to carry a dinky twenty-two, and with the tears runnin' down his cheeks begins to talk tall. Now what does that Cockeye do? Why, that pore kid that he had skinned couldn't 'a' hurt him with his pore little bric-à-brac. Does Cockeye take his little parlor ornament away from him, and spank him, and tell him to go home? No, he never. The kid's little tin pop-shooter explodes right in his hand before he can crook his forefinger twice, and while he's a-wondering what all has happened Cockeye gets his two guns on him, slow and deliberate like, mind you, and throws forty-eights into him till he ain't worth shooting at no more. Murders him like the mud-eating, horse-thieving snake of a Greaser that he is; but being within the law, the kid drawing on him first, he don't stretch hemp the way he should.

"Well, fin'ly this Blacklock blows into a mining camp in Placer County, California, where I'm chuck-tending on the night shift. This here camp is maybe four miles across the divide from Iowa Hill, and it sure is named a cu-roos name, which it is Why-not. They is a barn contiguous, where the mine horses are kep', and, blame me! if there ain't a weathercock on top of that same—a golden trotting horse—*upside down.* When the stranger an' pilgrim comes in, says he first off: 'Why'n snakes they got that weathercock horse upside down—why?' says he. 'Why-not,' says you, and the drinks is on the pilgrim.

"That all went very lovely till some gesabe opens up a placer drift on the far side the divide, starts a rival camp, an' names her Because. The Boss gets mad at that, and rights up the weathercock, and renames the camp Ophir, and you don't work no more pilgrims.

"Well, as I was saying, Cockeye drifts into Why-not and begins diffusing trouble. He skins some of the boys in the hotel over in town, and a big row comes of it, and one of the bedrock cleaners cuts loose with both guns. Nobody hurt but a quarter-breed, who loses a' eye. But the marshal don't stand for no short-card men, an' closes Cockeye up some prompt. Him being forced to give the boys back their money is busted an' can't get away from camp. To raise some wind he begins depredating.

"He robs a pore half-breed of a cayuse, and shoots up a Chink who's panning tailings, and generally and variously becomes too pronounced, till he's run outen camp. He's sure stony-broke, not being able to turn a card because of the marshal. So he goes to live in a' ole cabin up by the mine ditch, and sits there doing a heap o' thinking, and hatching trouble like a' ole he-hen.

"Well, now, with that deporting of Cockeye comes his turn of bad luck, and it sure winds his clock up with a loud report. I've narrated special of the scope and range of this 'ere Blacklock, so as you'll understand why it was expedient and desirable that he should up an' die. You see, he always managed, with all his killings and robbings and general and sundry flimflamming, to be just within the law. And if anybody took a notion to shoot him up, why, his luck saw him through, and the other man's shooting iron missed fire, or exploded, or threw wild, or such like, till it seemed as if he sure did bear a charmed life; and so he did till a pore yeller tamale of a fool dog did for him what the law of the land couldn't do. Yes, sir, a fool dog, a pup, a blame yeller pup named Sloppy Weather, did for Cockeye Blacklock, sporting character, three-card monte man, sure-thing sharp, killer, and general bedeviler.

"You see, it was this way. Over in American Canyon, some five miles maybe back of the mine, they was a creek called the American River, and it was sure chock-a-block full of trouts. The Boss used for to go over there with a dinky fish pole like a buggy whip about once a week, and scout that stream for fish and bring back a basketful. He was sure keen on it, and had bought some kind of privilege or other, so as he could keep other people off.

"Well, I used to go along with him to pack the truck, and one Saturday, about a month after Cockeye had been run outen camp, we hiked up over the divide, and went for to round up a bunch o' trouts. When we got to the river there was a mess for your life. Say, that river was full of dead trouts, floating atop the water; and they was some even on the bank. Not a scratch on 'em; just dead. The Boss had the papsy-lals. I never *did* see a man so rip-r'aring, snorting mad. *I* hadn't a guess about what we were up against, but he knew, and he showed down. He said somebody had been shooting the river for fish to sell down Sacramento way to the market. A mean trick; kill more fish in one shoot than you can possibly pack.

"Well, we didn't do much fishing that day—couldn't get a bite, for that matter—and took off home about noon to talk it over. You see, the Boss, in buying the privileges or such for that creek, had made himself responsible to the Fish Commissioners of the State, and 'twasn't a week before they were after him, camping on his trail incessant, and wanting to know how about it. The Boss was some worried, because the fish were being killed right along, and the Commission was making him weary of living. Twicet afterward we prospected along that river and found the same lot of dead fish. We even put a guard there, but it didn't do no manner of good.

"It's the Boss who first suspicions Cockeye. But it don't take no seventh daughter of no seventh daughter to trace trouble where Blacklock's about. He sudden shows up in town with a bunch of simoleons, buying bacon and tin cows* and such provender, and generally giving it away that he's come into money. The Boss, who's watching his movements sharp, says to me one day:

"'Bunt, the storm center of this here low area is a man with a Cockeye, an' I'll back that play with a paint horse against a paper dime.'

"'No takers,' says I. 'Dirty work and a Cockeyed man are two heels of the same mule.'

"'Which it's a-kicking of me in the stummick frequent and painful,' he remarks, plenty wrathful.

"'On general principles,' I said, 'it's a royal flush to a pair of deuces as how this Blacklock bird ought to stop a heap of lead, and I know the man to throw it. He's the only brother of my sister, and tends chuck in a placer mine. How about if I take a day off and drop round to his cabin and interview him on the fleetin' and unstable nature of human life?'

"But the Boss wouldn't hear of that.

"'No,' says he; 'that's not the bluff to back in this game. You an' me an' Mary-go-round'—that was what we called the marshal, him being so much all over the country—'you an' me an' Mary-go-round will have to stock a sure-thing deck against that maverick.'

* Condensed milk.

"So the three of us gets together an' has a talky-talk, an' we lays it out as how Cockeye must be watched and caught red-handed.

"Well, let me tell you, keeping case on that Greaser sure did lack a certain indefinable charm. We tried him at sunup, an' again at sundown, an' nights, too, laying in the chaparral an' tarweed, an' scouting up an' down that blame river, till we were sore. We built surreptitious a lot of shooting boxes up in trees on the far side of the canyon, overlooking certain an' sundry pools in the river where Cockeye would be likely to pursue operations, an' we took turns watching. I'll be a Chink if that bad egg didn't put it on us same as previous, an' we'd find new-killed fish all the time. I tell you we were *fitchered*; and it got on the Boss's nerves. The Commission began to talk of withdrawing the privilege, an' it was up to him to make good or pass the deal. We *knew* Blacklock was shooting the river, y' see, but we didn't have no evidence. Y' see, being shut off from cardsharping, he was up against it, and so took to pot hunting to get along. It was as plain as red paint.

"Well, things went along sort of catch-as-catch-can like this for maybe three weeks, the Greaser shooting fish regular, an' the Boss b'iling with rage, and laying plans to call his hand, and getting bluffed out every deal.

"And right here I got to interrupt, to talk some about the pup dog, Sloppy Weather. If he hadn't got caught up into this Blacklock game, no one'd ever thought enough about him to so much as kick him. But after it was all over, we began to remember this same Sloppy an' to recall what he was; no big job. He was just a worthless fool pup, yeller at that, everybody's dog, that just hung round camp, grinning and giggling and playing the goat, as half-grown dogs will. He used to go along with the car boys when they went swimmin' in the resevoy, an' dash along in an' yell an' splash round just to show off. He thought it was a keen stunt to get some gesabe to throw a stick in the resevoy so's he could paddle out after it. They'd trained him always to bring it back an' fetch it to whichever party throwed it. He'd give it up when he'd retrieved it, an' yell to have it throwed again. That was his idea of fun—just like a fool pup.

"Well, one day this Sloppy Weather is off chasing jackrabbits an' don't come home. Nobody thinks anything about that, nor even notices it. But we afterward finds out that he'd met up with

Blacklock that day, an' stopped to visit with him—sorry day for Cockeye. Now it was the very next day after this that Mary-go-round an' the Boss plans another scout. I'm to go, too. It was a Wednesday, an' we lay it out that the Cockeye would prob'ly shoot that day so's to get his fish down to the railroad Thursday, so they'd reach Sacramento Friday—fish day, see. It wasn't much to go by, but it was the high card in our hand, an' we allowed to draw to it.

"We left Why-not afore daybreak, an' worked over into the canyon about sunup. They was one big pool we hadn't covered for some time, an' we made out we'd watch that. So we worked down to it, an' clumb up into our trees, an' set out to keep guard.

"In about an hour we heard a shoot some mile or so up the creek. They's no mistaking dynamite, leastways not to miners, an' we knew that shoot was dynamite an' nothing else. The Cockeye was at work, an' we shook hands all round. Then pretty soon a fish or so began to go by—big fellows, some of 'em, dead an' floatin', with their eyes popped 'way out same as knobs—sure sign they'd been shot.

"The Boss took and grit his teeth when he see a three-pounder go by, an' made remarks about Blacklock.

"'Sh!' says Mary-go-round, sudden-like. 'Listen!'

"We turned ear down the wind, an' sure there was the sound of someone scrabbling along the boulders by the riverside. Then we heard a pup yap.

"'That's our man,' whispers the Boss.

"For a long time we thought Cockeye had quit for the day an' had coppered us again, but byne-by we heard the manzanita crack on the far side the canyon, an' there at last we see Blacklock working down toward the pool, Sloppy Weather following an' yapping and cayoodling just as a fool dog will.

"Blacklock comes down to the edge of the water quiet-like. He lays his big scoop net an' his sack—we can see it half full already—down behind a boulder, and takes a good squinting look all round, and listens maybe twenty minutes. He's that cute, same's a coyote stealing sheep. We lies low an' says nothing, fear he might see the leaves move.

"Then byne-by he takes his stick of dynamite out his hip pocket—he was just that reckless kind to carry it that way—an'

ties it careful to a couple of stones he finds handy. Then he lights
the fuse an' heaves her into the drink, an' just there's where
Cockeye makes the mistake of his life. He ain't tied the rocks tight
enough, an' the loop slips off just as he swings back his arm, the
stones drop straight down by his feet, and the stick of dynamite
whirls out right enough into the pool.

"Then the funny business begins.

"Blacklock ain't made no note of Sloppy Weather, who's been
sizing up the whole game an' watchin' for the stick. Soon as
Cockeye heaves the dynamite into the water, off goes the pup
after it, just as he'd been taught to do by the car boys.

"'Hey, you fool dog!' yells Blacklock.

"A lot that pup cares. He heads out for that stick of dynamite
same as if for a veal cutlet, reaches it, grabs hold of it, an' starts
back for shore, with the fuse sputterin' like hot grease. Blacklock
heaves rocks at him like one possessed, capering an' dancing; but
the pup comes right on. The Cockeye can't stand it no longer, but
lines out. But the pup's got to shore an' takes after him. Sure; why
not? He think's it's all part of the game. Takes after Cockeye, running to beat a' express, while we all whoops and yells an' nearly
falls out the trees for laffing. Hi! Cockeye did scratch gravel for
sure. But 'tain't no manner of use. He can't run through that
rough ground like Sloppy Weather, an' that fool pup comes
a-cavartin' along, jumpin' up against him, an' him a-kickin' him
away, an' r'arin', an' dancin', an' shakin' his fists, an' the more he
r'ars the more fun the pup thinks it is. But all at once something
big happens, an' the whole bank of the canyon opens out like a
big wave, and slops over into the pool, an' the air is full of trees
an' rocks and cartloads of dirt an' dogs and Blacklocks and rivers
an' smoke an' fire generally. The Boss got a clod o' river mud
spang in the eye, an' went off his limb like's he was trying to bust
a bucking bronc' an' couldn't; and ol' Mary-go-round was shooting off his gun on general principles, glarin' round wild-eyed an'
like as if he saw a' Injun devil.

"When the smoke had cleared away an' the trees and rocks
quit falling, we clumb down from our places an' started in to look
for Blacklock. We found a good deal of him, but they wasn't hide
nor hair left of Sloppy Weather. We didn't have to dig no grave,
either. They was a big enough hole in the ground to bury a horse

an' wagon, let alone Cockeye. So we planted him there, an' put up a board, an' wrote on it:

Here lies most
of
C. BLACKLOCK,
who died of a'
entangling alliance with
a
stick of dynamite.

Moral: A hook and line is good enough
fish tackle for any honest man.

"That there board lasted for two years, till the freshet of '82, when the American River—— Hello, there's the sun!"

All in a minute the night seemed to have closed up like a great book. The East flamed roseate. The air was cold, nimble. Some of the sagebrush bore a thin rim of frost. The herd, aroused, the dew glistening on flank and horn, were chewing the first cud of the day, and in twos and threes moving toward the water hole for the morning's drink. Far off toward the camp the breakfast fire sent a shaft of blue smoke straight into the moveless air. A jackrabbit, with erect ears, limped from the sagebrush just out of pistol shot and regarded us a moment, his nose wrinkling and trembling. By the time that Bunt and I, putting our ponies to a canter, had pulled up by the camp of the Bar-circle-Z outfit, another day had begun in Idaho.

"No—certainly. Yes. Exactly—oh, precisely, sir. I know him—know him as well as any man knows another. Next to me he's about the best wheelsman aboard. And I'd hate to lose him. And—see here. I'm telling you this in confidence—but there's something wrong with you, boys. Two years ago he was a Methody preacher in Santa Clara. Well, he went on a tear, a revivalist, and he was hauling forth his blessed hot sermon in the sun when all to once he goes down. Him, an' don't come round for the better part o' two days. When he woke up, he's another person; he's forgot the name, forgot his job, forgot the whole blamed shooting match. And he hain't never remembered it since. He's had this here thing for the load o' thing, however it does happen now and again. Well, he turned to and began sailoring like off—now, as the old mate and me was done with him—oh, him not having any friends, so you might say, he was let go his own gait. He got to be third mate o' some kind o' Bangladesh down Mexico way; and then I got hold o' him an' took him into the company. He's been with me ever since. He ain't got the faintest kind o' recollection o' his Methody days, an' believes he's always been a sailorman. Well, that's his business, ain't it? If he takes my orders an' walks chalk, what do I care about his Methody spree? There, boys, is the original, history and development of Slick Dick Nickerson. If you take on this sea-otter deal and go to Point Barrow, naturally Nick has got to go as owner's agent and representative of the Company. But I couldn't send an easier fellow to get along with. Honest, now, I couldn't. Boys, you think over the proposition between now and tomorrow an' then come around and let me know."

And the upshot of the whole matter was that one month later the Bertha Millner, with Dickerson, Hardenberg, Strokher and Ally Bazan on board, cleared from San Francisco, bound—the papers were beautifully precise—for Seattle and Tacoma with a cargo of general merchandise.

As a matter of fact, the bulk of her cargo consisted of some odd hundreds of very fine lumps of rock—which as ballast is cheap by the ton—and some odd dozen cases of conspicuously labeled champagne.

The Pacific and Oriental Flotation Company made this champagne out of Rhine wine, effervescent salts, raisins, rock candy

Bibliography

Yvernelle (1892) - narrative poem
Moran of the Lady Letty (1898) - novel
McTeague (1899) - novel
Blix (1899) - novel
A Man's Woman (1900) - novel
The Octopus (1901) - novel
The Pit (1903) - novel
The Responsibilities of the Novelist (1903) - essays
A Deal in Wheat (1903) - short stories
The Joyous Miracle (1906) - tale
The Third Circle (1909) - short stories
Vandover and the Brute (1914) - novel
The Surrender of Santiago (1917) - nonfiction: history
The Argonaut Manuscript Limited Edition of Frank Norris's Works
(1928) - collected works
Frank Norris of "The Wave" (1931) - stories and sketches
The Letters of Frank Norris (1956) - selected letters
The Literary Criticism of Frank Norris (1964) - essays

Original Publication Source
of the Short Stories

1. The Jongleur of Taillebois: *Wave* December 25, 1891
2. A Defense of the Flag: *Argonaut* October 28, 1895
3. His Sister: *Wave* November 28, 1896
4. Man Proposes — No. I: *Wave* May 23, 1896
             No. II: *Wave* May 30, 1896
             No. III: *Wave* June 13, 1896
             No. IV: *Wave* June 27, 1896
             No. V: *Wave* July 4, 1896
5. Judy's Service of Gold Plate: *Wave* October 16, 1897
6. Shorty Stack, Pugilist: *Wave* November 20, 1897
7. The Third Circle: *Wave* August 28, 1897
8. Buldy Jones, *Chef de Claque*: *Everybody's Magazine* May 1901
9. A Deal in Wheat: *Everybody's Magazine* August 1902